THE SHADOWING

BOOK TWO

SKINNED

ADAM SLATER

EGMONT
USA
NEW YORK

With special thanks to Elizabeth Wein

EGMONT
We bring stories to life

First published in the United Kingdom by Egmont UK Ltd, 2011
First published in the United States of America by Egmont USA, 2012
443 Park Avenue South, Suite 806
New York, NY 10016

1 3 5 7 9 8 6 4 2

www.egmontusa.com

Library of Congress Cataloging-in-Publication Data

Slater, Adam.
Skinned / Adam Slater.
p.   cm. — (The Shadowing ; #2)
Summary: Destined to guard the Boundary between the mortal world
and the Netherworld, teenaged Callum must stop a flesh-eating
monster from luring young children into her lair.
ISBN 978-1-60684-262-1 (hardcover) — ISBN 978-1-60684-381-9 (e-book)
[1. Demonology—Fiction. 2. Supernatural—Fiction.
3. Fate and fatalism—Fiction.] I. Title.
PZ7.S62895Sk 2012   [Fic]—dc23   2012012542

Printed in the United States of America

Prologue

There aren't any trees in the little circular cul-de-sac where the boy lives, but there is a tall, wooden telephone pole, sprouting a wire into each house in the street. Every night before bed, the boy checks to see if there are any birds perched on the wire that ties the pole to his own house. Sometimes on winter nights there are stars framed between them. Tonight there is a full moon. The boy leans his elbows on the windowsill and stares, imagining flying off in a spaceship.

Then, suddenly, the night twists.

It is the oddest thing the boy has ever seen. The

view from his window warps for a moment, as though reflected in a wobbly mirror at a funfair. The air between the cable and the ground seems to break and reform, the way still water ripples and then settles when you touch it.

The boy rubs his eyes. He shakes his head before he looks again to see if the ripple is still there.

It isn't. Instead, there is a woman standing on the pavement.

In the pale light of the full moon, the woman's skin is faintly blue, as though she has been nearly frozen to death. Around her shoulders is a tattered shawl, too full of holes to protect against the winter air. Her ragged leather skirt doesn't look very warm either.

Where did she come from?

The boy at the window is fascinated. He can't look away.

*

Black Annis lifts her head, swivels her eyes first one way and then the other. Above her stands a wooden mast with thick, black ropes stretching out to the strange houses around it. Beneath her feet, the ground is as hard as rock.

The world has changed.

When she last crossed over and walked this land, it was field and forest. Now all that is gone. No trees anywhere — only this bare wooden pole. Gone, too, the entrance to the cave Black Annis scratched from the sandstone of Dane's Hill with her own nails. Gone, the oak that grew at its mouth, where she hung out the flayed skins of her victims to dry so that later she might sew them for her skirts.

And what is that smell — thick and acrid? It surrounds her, dulling the cold, fresh scent of night and the aroma of warm, living things. All changed, all gone — nothing remains of what Black Annis knew in this world. It is buried beneath this grey layer of grit and tar, and row upon row of smoky human dwellings. For a moment, in the cavity where her shrivelled, inhuman heart beats, Black Annis knows something like despair.

Then her eyes follow one of the black ropes overhead. It stretches from the top of the tall, wooden pole to the bottom of a window. And in the window, moonlight shining on his white face, there is a child.

Black Annis smiles. Her pointed teeth do not gleam; they are black with age and the bloodstains of her countless victims. But they are still strong, still primed for their purpose. She looks up at the human child — surely meant to be in bed and asleep at this time of night.

Some things never change.

*

The boy watches as the cold woman turns her head, looking up at the telephone pole, and finally looking at him. Straight at him. Her eyes seem alight, glinting brightly. Her lips pull back over teeth that make a dark stain in the middle of her pale, bluish face.

It is a smile. She sees him.

Now he notices something else. Her arms seem too long for her body, and her fingers – no one can have fingers that long! Unless . . . Were they her *fingernails*?

The boy snaps out of his trance, all fascination instantly turned to fear. He backs away from the window.

*

4

Black Annis walks towards the house. Inside the gate, separating the building from the hard grey ground beyond, there is a tiny patch of grass and earth. The soil here has not changed. The sandy loam is soft and familiar. It is good to feel the earth beneath her feet again.

Black Annis reaches the house and looks up. It is bigger than the human dwelling places she remembers. The windows are higher.

But her nails are as sharp as ever they were. She is good at climbing.

*

Cowering away from the window, the boy can see nothing. But he can hear an odd noise outside – a scratching beneath the window, growing steadily louder. The boy doesn't want to look, but he has to know what it is.

He forces himself back to the window. He grips the sill and peers out across the street. The strange woman is gone.

But the noise is still growing louder. The boy looks

down at the window ledge outside the house. Long, sharp claws are hooked into the wood. As the boy watches, the dark claws flex and grip. Behind them rise long, pale arms, blue in the night's half-light. The arms haul up the rest of the grotesque body. Black teeth and silver eyes rise into view, filling the window.

*

Black Annis is face to face with her victim. Her grin widens. The human child dashes across the room, throws himself into his bed and dives under the covers. Black Annis can see the heap of human helplessness trembling beneath the flimsy cloth and down.

The boy's terror is delicious.

*

Under his duvet, the boy hides, his nerves a snarled tangle of despair and hope. Surely he is safe here. The blue woman can't see him any more, and the window is shut tight –

6

Click.

The sound is soft and sudden. A cold draught of night air reaches under the covers and stings the boy's trembling ankles. The window is open.

The child waits, his heart pounding with fear, as he listens to the quiet, slow footfalls padding across his bedroom floor. Then they stop, and the boy holds his breath, waiting . . . Perhaps she's gone? Perhaps it was all his imagination, perhaps –

There is no more warning. The covers are ripped from his body in one lightning sweep. It is too late for him to scream for help.

He screams anyway.

Chapter One

Evening had well and truly settled in Nether Marlock, and Callum stared out of his bedroom window at the night sky. He knew he should be concentrating on his English homework, but these days it didn't take much to distract him. He could hear Gran downstairs cleaning their small cottage vigorously. At least she'd found something to occupy her mind, he thought. Sighing, Callum rubbed his eyes. He cracked open his bedroom window a little to get some fresh air, and then looked back down at his textbook.

A moment later, he heard a noise. At first he thought it was a branch of the rowan tree that grew next to the ramshackle alms cottage, scratching at the top of the window. But when he looked up, Callum saw bones not branches. Fluttering at the glass was a bird, the size of a crow, but not like any he had ever seen.

It was a skeleton.

The bird's bony wings rattled and battered insistently against the window pane. Callum held his breath. He had always been able to see ghosts – they were such an ordinary part of his life that when he'd been younger he had sometimes confused them with the living. There was no confusing this thing, though – whether it was a ghost or not, it was certainly no ordinary bird. And it was obviously determined to get his attention.

Before Callum could even react, the skeletal creature suddenly swooped downwards and hurtled through the open window into the room. The clattering bones landed on his desk in a jumbled heap. Shock strangled Callum's voice in his throat as the bone crow reformed itself in a swirl of icy wind. It opened its beak in a long, silent caw. Its breath smelled like mould. The crow flicked its bare skull back towards the window as though it was beckoning Callum, and with a flourish of featherless wings it swooped back to the windowsill, daring him to follow it outside.

'What the . . .?' Callum began in a shaky whisper, but then stopped. He'd learned by now not to ignore supernatural commands, however strange or disturbing they might be. He knew that he had a role to play in the bizarre events that had become a part of his daily life.

Callum quickly made his way down the narrow spiral stairs to the little sitting room, pulling on a hooded sweatshirt and then his jacket. 'I'm going for a walk,' he called quickly to his grandmother, who was still doing the washing up in the kitchen.

'It's freezing out there. What on earth would you want to do that for?' she replied.

Callum grimaced. He'd been hoping for a quick getaway, but lately Gran had been watching him like a hawk.

'You ought to be careful now, Callum,' she continued, drying off her hands and then folding her arms in concern.

'I just need to get some fresh air, that's all,' he said. Gran raised her eyebrows, but before she could say anything more, Callum had slipped through the front door and out into the icy evening.

He scanned the dark sky, and saw the skeleton crow circling overhead. Glancing back briefly at the cottage, through the open curtains of the sitting room window he could see the new set of sliding glass doors that led to the back garden. He shivered, and not just from the aching cold.

Callum still couldn't look at the glass without remembering the awful battle with the Fetch. He could still picture the horrendous skinless 'face' of the evil demon that had hunted him so recently. Those doors had been shattered during the struggle, but Gran had got them fixed as soon as she possibly could, smoothing things over as if nothing had ever happened. *All part of her disguise*, Callum thought. Her plan to make sure everything seemed *normal*.

But she's a witch, Callum reminded himself. And she always has been.

Anger briefly warmed him, and his face flushed as

he remembered the secrets that had unravelled only weeks ago: all the protective spells Gran had been weaving to conceal Callum's true nature not only from himself, but from the Netherworld and its terrible demons. His grandmother had been hiding the truth from him for *years*, and Callum had had no idea.

There was no avoiding it now, though. He was a chime child.

'*Child*,' he muttered to himself wryly, his breath pluming into the air. It seemed like there was an awful lot of expectation on someone referred to as a kid. Chime children were those born under a full moon between midnight on Friday and cockcrow on Saturday morning; the chime hours. They were destined to guard the Boundary between the mortal world and the Netherworld until they turned eighteen. Seeing ghosts and other weird stuff, like the bone crow, was just one of the 'gifts' that was meant to help in this task. But after the Fetch's spree of gory assassinations, Callum was the only chime child left alive.

The crow's bones clattered as it dived down in front of him and Callum jerked away from it as its thin, white wings passed in front of his face.

'All right, I'm coming,' Callum whispered, his voice shaking in spite of himself. He wasn't sure he really wanted to follow. Part of him would have rather pretended that none of this was happening, that he could just go back to his room in the cottage, with Gran fussing and bustling around him.

But she lied to me, he thought fiercely. If it hadn't been for the Fetch turning up, Callum might still not know he *was* a chime child. And he certainly wouldn't know about his father, who'd vanished mysteriously before Callum was born. He had been a chime child too. Callum found it strangely comforting that his dad had been through some of what he was about to face.

He shivered as the wind picked up, moving his hands from his pockets and tucking them up into his armpits. He'd left in such a hurry he hadn't bothered with gloves. Winter seemed to be coming even earlier this year. At least he could be sure that Gran would have the cottage warm when he finally got back home. He sighed. She was Callum's whole family now – she had been for the past three years since his mum had died. Deep down, he knew that by keeping him in the dark she had only been trying to protect him from what he must now face.

The Shadowing.

Callum felt uncomfortable even thinking the phrase. All he really knew was that it happened once every hundred years, and that during the thirteen moons of the Shadowing, the Boundary between worlds would grow weaker, allowing an untold number of nightmarish beasts to cross over into the mortal world. Callum wasn't sure if he was ready for what was to come. After all, the Fetch was only the beginning.

His eyes darted up to the sky once more as the skeleton crow swooped down and opened its beak for its strange, silent caw. An enormous full moon sailed high in the sky, casting crystalline light over Nether Marlock Road. As Callum reached the woods, he saw that the trees were white with frost, standing in quiet ranks like an army of dead soldiers. Their peculiar glow lit his way. The sound of his trudging through the frozen silence was making him increasingly tense, but stealth was impossible. Each step made the hard frost crackle like a fire.

Callum stopped suddenly. Was that a twig snapping *behind* him? He whirled round, his heart racing, his eyes darting left and right. He stood still for a long while but, hearing nothing else, he decided it must have been an echo of his own footsteps. Callum's jaw clenched, but he didn't allow himself another shiver. Now was not the time to be nervous. He buried his hands further into his pockets as he walked. Callum had a suspicion now that he knew where they were going, and who may have sent the sinister messenger to summon him . . .

Sure enough, a few moments later, Callum finally reached the lane that led to the ruins of Nether Marlock Church. There, by the iron gate that led into the old churchyard – one of the most haunted places in Marlock – a silhouette made a dark shape against the vivid light of the huge, round moon. Callum's muscles tensed, and he held his breath as he peered through the gloom, trying to make out the stranger's face . . .

He exhaled in relief. 'What the hell are *you* doing here?'

'Nice to see you too,' came Melissa's reply.

'Sorry,' Callum answered, taking another deep, calming breath before he spoke to his friend. 'You just weren't who I was expecting.'

'I know,' Melissa said softly. 'But look.'

She held up her hand.

Perched on her wrist was a little skeleton bird, a bit like the crow that had come banging against Callum's window, but this one was the size of a sparrow.

'It's creepy, but it seems to *like* me,' Melissa said. 'I have to keep pushing it off because it makes my arm so cold after a couple of minutes.'

'Melissa, seriously, what are you doing here?'

'This thing wanted me to follow it, so I did. Just like you, it seems . . .' She pointed to the crow skeleton. 'Wow, that thing's *big*. I'd have died of fright if Jacob had sent me one of *those*.'

Callum smiled a little. If there was anyone who would be willing to get involved in all the crazy supernatural stuff going on in his life, it was Melissa. He was amazed at how she just took all these things in her stride – even Jacob. Any normal person who

16

encountered a Born Dead ghost would have run a million miles. But not her. Spooky might as well be Melissa's middle name.

She shook her arm to get the skeleton sparrow off her wrist. *'Shoo.'* The creature flew off, but the two strange birds paid no attention to each other – just fluttered in mid-air above Callum and Melissa's heads, the white bones of their wings clattering noisily. Callum's crow gave another silent, mould-scented scream and flapped away into the darkness towards the entrance to the ruined church.

'Better follow,' Callum said grimly. 'Jacob must have brought us both here for a reason.'

It was darker in the churchyard than it had been on the road. Callum knew from experience that if he didn't take care, he'd trip over tombstones or the iron railings marking Victorian graves and end up flat on his face. The church loomed like an ice-bound ship, faintly etched in frost.

'Can't see anything,' said Melissa. 'Maybe he's not here –?'

The doorway of the church was suddenly swallowed

in darkness. Callum and Melissa stumbled against each other as a rope of wind even chillier than the night itself wound around their legs. White, gleaming fangs flashed in the middle of the inky shadow in the door, and a terrifying rumble reverberated around the cemetery as the enormous beast let rip a supernatural canine growl.

It was Doom, the Churchyard Grim and Jacob's companion.

The giant dog loomed in the ruined doorway, fangs bared. Now he backed away – an invitation to proceed. Gritting his teeth, Callum went first, and Melissa followed. He hadn't always trusted Doom, but Callum couldn't deny that it was his icy fangs that destroyed the Fetch. The spectral dog was on their side, or at least seemed to be . . .

Doom turned and loped into the church after them, the bone-birds darting about his great shadowy form.

'Jacob?'

Callum's voice echoed inside the cold, ruined walls of the sanctuary. He and Melissa stood still, side by side, peering at the jagged shadows thrown in all directions by the light of the soaring moon outside.

They had both been there before, and it was never exactly a settling experience, but this felt different. For Jacob to summon the two of them here so late in the evening must mean something serious.

As Callum's eyes adjusted to the gloom, he realised that Jacob was already there. The ghost-boy stood just beside the ruined altar in his long black coat, fingers clenched, hands by his sides. Longish, black hair shadowed his faintly gleaming skin.

Doom moved to stand next to his master, and Callum saw Jacob's pale hand reach up to grip the dark fur at the back of Doom's neck.

Suddenly, there came a tremendous flash of lightning, which tore the night in two and caused Callum to stagger back in shock. For one second he could see everything as though in broad, clear daylight – every stone of the ruined church, every leaf of ivy and stem of nettle winding among the stones picked out in perfect detail – the bird skeletons in mid-air, the spectral figures of Jacob and Doom, starkly outlined in black and glowing silver. Then the light was gone and Callum could see nothing.

But he heard Jacob's echoing, bell-like voice cut through the darkness.

'The Shadowing has begun.'

Chapter Two

Callum could feel Jacob's eyes fixed on him expectantly.

'Well, what do you want me to say?' he asked.

Things didn't feel any different – there was no sudden change, no flood of demonic energy. Just the bone-trembling cold. Jacob pointed towards the ruined wall of the church, through the space a window would once have been, and towards the night sky. His finger dripped with the black blood that often seeped from his fingernails.

'This,' the ghost began, 'is merely the first moon of the thirteen. The full force of the Shadowing is not immediate. But that does not mean we are able to linger. Already, there is much danger.'

Melissa looked over at Callum, then to Jacob. 'Well, it's all a bit of an anti-climax so far,' she said with a tentative grin. But Callum couldn't bring himself to smile.

'What do you mean, the full force is not immediate?' he said.

'When the Shadowing commences, the floodgates do not simply open,' Jacob said. 'The Boundary between the mortal world and the Netherworld remains in place but, as the cycle of the moons progresses, there will be a steady increase in the number of gaps in its fabric.'

Callum cleared his throat.

'And the more weak points there are in the Boundary, the more . . . *stuff* . . . can cross over from the Netherworld?'

'That is correct,' Jacob said grimly. 'The situation will grow more and more perilous. Indeed, it is already dangerous. From this night forward, demons and other beings of the Netherworld – ghosts, creatures of mortal legend, murderous beasts – they will all begin to surface with increasing frequency in the world of men. They will be set on destruction and feasting, on fear and on flesh.' He paused, looking at Callum and Melissa closely. 'The threat will escalate through the thirteen moons. But during this dark time of the Shadowing, *you*, Callum . . .' The ghost trailed off for a moment, his expression becoming something close to regretful. 'You will be the Boundary's final guardian. You are the last chime child.'

Callum nodded mutely, straining his ears and eyes, half expecting to see goblins begin to pop out of the stonework, or through the gaping black hole of the tower door. Suddenly realising he had been holding his breath, he exhaled it in a gust and shook his head.

'Well, what can I do?' Callum asked. He was surprised to feel a sense of urgency and purpose overtaking him. 'Can I do anything to slow it down, prevent the crossings, limit them? Or –'

Jacob held up one pale hand. 'We must not get ahead of ourselves. Of course, your aim will be to guard the Boundary, to prevent Netherworld beings from crossing and to combat those that do. But now that this job falls on your shoulders alone, we must have a plan of action.' Jacob pushed his black hair out of his face.

'But usually there would be a whole *army* of chime children. How on earth can Callum police *all* the weakening points in the Boundary on his own, especially if there will be more and more appearing all the time?' Melissa asked.

Jacob was silent for a moment before he spoke again. 'Callum will have to be selective about the battles he takes on. As the Shadowing progresses, stronger and more significant demons and beasts will cross into the mortal world. Those will be the ones on which Callum should focus.'

'So for now, he'll just have to leave whatever smaller demons make it across? Just let them slide?' Melissa said, her eyebrows raised.

'I'll just have to do the very best that I can,' Callum said, lifting his head and trying to sound confident.

Jacob gave what, for the Born Dead, was close to a smile. 'Good. As I say, we still have some time before the worst of the Shadowing begins. We must use that time wisely, growing and honing your innate abilities.'

'Right,' Callum said. 'And . . . what exactly *are* my abilities? I mean, I already know that I can stop ghosts or demons from entering Gran's cottage. Somehow I have that ability to raise a barrier, to stop them from crossing my threshold unless they're invited, right? So maybe . . .' He paused, still not used to all this. He felt faintly idiotic using the word *magic*. 'Is there some sort of supercharged version that I could do for the entire world?'

Jacob answered Callum's question with another. 'How did the Fetch cross the barrier into your house?'

'It got Gran to invite it in,' Callum said, and then sighed as the thought sunk in. 'Great. So even if I had some sort of protective force field on the Boundary, someone else might get round that and invite things across of their own accord?'

Jacob nodded. 'There's almost certainly some form of collaboration going on between your world and the Netherworld. The Fetch could not have come over to this side before the Shadowing had begun without help. And with the assassination of the chime children, this Shadowing is not like others that have taken place. It is more than just a weakening of the Boundary. It could be an invasion. A *war*. I believe the demons are working with their human conspirators to take over this world forever.'

Silence fell after Jacob's words. His face was serious. In the darkness, Callum could see faint lines of shadow crease against Jacob's gleaming white forehead. It wasn't exactly filling him with confidence.

'There's one thing you mustn't forget though,' Melissa put in. Callum turned to look at her quizzically. He'd almost forgotten she was there.

'Yeah?' he said, pleased to break the tension.

'Callum, you're *strong*. Maybe even the strongest of all the chime children that were active before the Shadowing began,' Melissa said emphatically. 'How else do you explain that you're the one still alive? You may not quite have a handle on all your powers yet, but I just have this feeling that you shouldn't be underestimated.' She paused, and a glimmer of a grin began to flicker on her lips. 'And there's one other thing they haven't counted on,' she said.

'What's that?' Callum asked.

'Me and Jacob.'

Jacob stared at Melissa with some surprise, and Callum could see something like respect in his face. Melissa stood shivering in the dark, but wide-eyed and alert.

'Seriously, I'll do whatever I can to help.'

'It will not be easy,' Jacob said, nodding to acknowledge Melissa. 'You have only just learned your power exists, Callum. We do have some time, but we also have a distance to go. You are going to have to master your abilities, and you are going to have to do it under a degree of pressure.'

'How exactly *will* I master them?'

'I will teach you. Do not forget that although I died at birth, I too am a chime child.'

Callum nodded. He would have been lost without Jacob's help when the Fetch had reared its hideous head only weeks ago. He looked at Jacob again, who was staring at Callum pointedly.

'What, you want to teach me *now*? Here, in the dark?'

'No time like the present,' Jacob replied.

27

Again, Callum glanced at Melissa. She nodded once in encouragement.

'OK,' Callum said. 'What do I have to do?'

Jacob didn't answer him. Instead, he raised one white hand and pointed towards Callum.

'Doom.'

Without warning, the great black Grim leaped for Callum. The last thing Callum saw before he shut his eyes were the ghost dog's teeth, flashing like icicles as Doom opened his jaws . . .

Chapter Three

The whole thing happened in the blink of an eye.

Callum was knocked over by the force of the dog's attack. The Grim's body was so cold it took his breath away, sucking the air from his lungs and leaving them screaming for oxygen. He writhed desperately as the dog's breath washed over him, the hot stench of rotting meat making his stomach churn. Somewhere in the background he heard Melissa scream. Callum could feel Doom's weight on him, heavy as a pile of rocks. He lay there, his eyes squeezed shut, waiting for the inevitable – for those glittering, razor-sharp fangs to sink into his throat. But the shadow-dog held him pinned fast to the floor of the ruined church, his growl rumbling menacingly. Callum was sure his blood was turning to ice in his veins. He knew he was foolish to have ever trusted the beast, or to have believed that Jacob wouldn't betray him. *Oh, please, just let it be over* . . .

'Release.'

Jacob's voice came from somewhere above them. Suddenly the crushing frigid weight on Callum's chest disappeared. His breath came out in a shivering rush. Doom stalked away from him and went to guard the church entrance once more.

Callum sat up slowly, quaking, and not with cold. Melissa was watching, and she wrapped her arms around herself quickly, as if the deathly chill of Doom's lunge had taken her own breath away as well. But Jacob's white face was neutral.

'That scared you,' he remarked.

Callum leaped to his feet angrily.

'Oh, well done!' he said, his voice tight. 'It's a pitch black winter's night. It's freezing, I'm surrounded by ghosts in an abandoned church in the middle of an ancient graveyard. My world is about to be invaded by monsters and demons, which apparently I'm responsible for dealing with. Do you think you need to do anything *more* to scare me?'

Jacob held Callum's gaze. 'Mastering your fear is very important. Indeed, many creatures of the Netherworld feed on it – they hunger for it, and they evoke it in their victims because the deeper and wilder the fear, the more satisfying the conquest. Fear *weakens* and *destabilises*. Recall how Doom made you wait, lying beneath his giant weight – your fear was growing all that time. If he'd meant to destroy you he would have continued his torment, until your mounting fear was at its peak, and only then would he have chosen his moment to finish the job. And so –'

'So what?' Callum shouted. 'So how does this help *at all*? This is insane. I have to get out of here . . .'

Melissa suddenly interrupted.

'Callum.'

He spun toward her with the same desperate fury he'd been focusing on Jacob.

'Calm down,' Melissa said.

Callum began to retort, but then took a breath and frowned, folding his arms defensively.

'That's the whole point, isn't it?' Melissa continued. 'You've got to calm down. As long as you're in control of yourself –'

'Your friend is right,' Jacob interjected. 'Your first challenge, and your most critical, is in facing your enemies calmly. It is the best hope of any soldier in any army. You've got to *control your fear*.'

'Riiiiight. No problem.' Callum couldn't keep the sarcasm from his voice – but a part of him also grudgingly acknowledged that the argument made sense.

'This is a lesson,' said Jacob. 'Nothing more. My intention is not to frighten you. I want you to *learn*.'

Callum sighed, which Jacob seemed to take as acceptance.

'Good,' he said.

With no more warning than that, Doom ran at Callum once more.

This time, the phantom hound halted in front of Callum with his fierce jaws gaping, and instead of making contact, put his head up and howled. The sound, like the scream of steel on steel, tore through Callum's head until he felt his skull was going to split in two.

Callum spun round and tried to scramble up the dark, ivy-covered stones sticking out of the church wall he was backed against, with no plan other than to get himself away from Doom's savage, howling jaws. The Grim was after him in less than a second. With a snarl, he snatched Callum by the back of his coat. The lethal, ice-white teeth brushed against his neck, their cold so fierce it instantly made his head ache like it had been packed in ice cubes. Doom yanked Callum away from the wall and threw him to the ground with a thud that made his bones rattle.

Control his fear? It felt impossible. Callum tried to steel himself as Doom's otherworldly growl echoed around them – he was sure any moment the grim would strike again.

Then, at Jacob's word, Doom became docile. He stepped away from Callum's gasping form and returned to his master's side.

Callum clenched his fists as he scrambled to his feet.

His annoyance was growing – but to his surprise, it was not with Jacob, or Doom, but with himself. He *knew* Doom was going to attack again, and he was *almost* certain that the great Churchyard Grim had no real intention of harming him. So it was pointless for Callum to allow himself to be so easily intimidated. He took a deep breath.

'All right,' he said, this time through gritted teeth. 'Again.'

The beast began to stalk towards him, fangs flashing.

Calm, Callum told himself – *stay CALM. Don't move, don't think, don't be afraid –*

Suddenly, in the split second before the Grim pounced again, Callum felt a tingling force begin to radiate from the core of his body and down his arms to his hands. It was similar to the sensation he felt when he was about to have a premonition of the future, the feeling he called his Luck, when the warning numbness in his hands told him danger lay ahead. But the odd thing was, now this tingling was channelling *through* and *out* of him – like electricity. It was faint, but he was throwing off some kind of energy, some kind of current –

Doom flew towards him, but it was different this time. Callum moved his hands out in front of him, and the Grim was knocked off course somehow, as though the energy from the weak static Callum was generating had deflected him. Only one icy forepaw thumped Callum in the shoulder – but it was still enough to knock him flat on his back into the nettles.

'Yes,' Jacob said, nodding his approval. 'Better.'

Doom sauntered over to lie at Jacob's feet again.

Callum turned to Melissa. 'Did you see anything?'

She shook her head – he could see only the movement in the dim light, not her expression. 'What did you do?' Melissa asked. 'What happened?'

'It was like – it felt like a little fizzle of energy, electricity, coming out of my hands,' Callum said, his voice breathless with excitement. 'Sort of like when my Luck tells me something bad is about to happen, but . . . stronger.'

'It is a beginning,' Jacob said. 'You are shaping. With practice – with *focus*, you will be able to channel that energy. The feeling you have had in your hands has always been a signal of this power waiting to be released. It is part of your chime child abilities, and you can use it, as you just did, to make a barrier. A shield. And with further effort you will also be able to use that energy . . . offensively.'

Callum raised his eyebrows. 'Sounds good,' he said with a grin.

'Sounds *really* good!' Melissa added eagerly.

'It takes some learning,' Jacob said, holding his hands out to caution them, though a smile played on his lips as well. 'Still, it is not so different from the barrier you were able to put up to protect the threshold of your house, Callum. Eventually you will be able to create it anywhere. There are other skills that will serve you in this war, other skills you can learn to master, but this is the first.' Jacob paused. 'It will not be easy.'

'I'll work,' said Callum through his teeth.

'Every day,' Jacob said. It wasn't a question.

There was *no doubt* it wouldn't be easy. But Callum realised now that he didn't have much choice. 'Every day,' he agreed. 'I'll be here. We can do it on my way to and from school – I'll leave early and come home late –'

Melissa interrupted again, her voice still eager.

'What can *I* do?'

She was no longer shivering. She, too, was standing with her fists clenched firmly by her sides, battling the cold as fiercely as Callum had been battling his fear.

'With your knowledge of supernatural folklore, I want you to take charge of a different branch of Callum's schooling,' Jacob said. 'While I can teach him how to control his powers, there is much history that he should have learnt by now. The lore of the chime child should have been passed down to Callum through the collection of books left to him by his father. At thirteen years of age, he should be close to knowing these books off by heart. But as his grandmother kept them hidden from him for so long, Callum no longer has the time to study them himself.'

'And?'

'You know something about these mysteries already,' Jacob told Melissa. 'You are well on your way to knowing as much as Callum ought. We need you to read the books – to learn and retain as much about their content as you possibly can, and to pass this knowledge on to Callum.'

Melissa's eyes narrowed sceptically. Callum could see her disbelief even in the dark, and it came as no surprise that she protested.

'That's not much of a challenge,' Melissa said doubtfully.

'He's right though, Melissa. You spend half your time reading books about practically anything to do with the supernatural anyway, right? It could really be helpful.'

Jacob nodded. 'Callum is lucky to have you as his source. You can make up for his lost time – add your existing knowledge to the wealth of information that Callum's father left him.'

'Fine. I'll do that,' Melissa said. 'But can't I do something else too? Why bring me here otherwise? Can't I do something a bit more . . . I don't know, a bit more *active*?'

'It is too dangerous,' Jacob said shortly.

'But I can learn things too,' she said. 'Ordinary

people have fought against the Netherworld before, surely?' She lifted her arm, and the bone sparrow that Jacob had sent her darted to land on her wrist. 'I mean, I have a head start. I've been interacting with the Netherworld, I have some idea what to expect – it can't be that big a leap for me to do something more than reading a couple of books?'

'It is a *war*, Melissa,' he stated flatly. 'Only those with power can take on the Netherworld.'

Mclissa dropped her hand so suddenly that the bone bird lost its balance and fell to the frozen ground with a clatter. It recovered itself and fluttered back to hover by her shoulder. She folded her arms. Perhaps she was cold again, but to Callum it looked distinctly like she was sulking.

'Fine, I'll be one of those women watching from sidelines while the men head off into battle, shall I? I'll read Callum's dusty books. But what exactly am I supposed to do, just march up to Callum's gran and say, "Hi, can I borrow those ancient tomes of chime child lore?"'

Jacob's gaze was steady. 'I do not believe she would

mind, now that she knows you are on her side – that you share her goals to protect and aid Callum.'

Jacob turned to Callum. 'Tell your grandmother that is why you came out tonight – to meet Melissa, so she can collect the books and read them for you. But best not to tell her you have been talking to a ghost.'

'Yeah, I think that's a given,' Callum said with a smile, but Jacob's face was serious.

'Your grandmother has been protecting you from the Netherworld all your life,' he said. 'Finally, she is beginning to accept the path you must take. But she is fearful for your safety and somehow I do not think she would be too pleased if she hears a Born Dead and a Grim are teaching you to use your chime child powers. In any discussion of your training, and indeed in all matters, I think it best not to mention me at all . . .'

Chapter Four

The corridor is dark and wet. Black Annis drags a solid, bulky load along the new passage she has tunnelled into the ground. The sandstone walls are streaked with clay, and the smell is of earth and roots and mould. She needs no light to navigate her way; she is at home underground. Her glowing eyes penetrate the darkness effortlessly. It feels good to be deep in the earth. She is certain hers are the only feet to have trodden this damp course in five hundred years and more. The path leads to her old lair.

Black Annis pauses, resting. The burden she drags along behind her is slowing her down, and having crossed at the first weakening point of the Boundary, she needs time to adjust to being back in the mortal world. She is a long way from her full strength, but she knows it is only a matter of time before it is restored.

It is good to be back in the world of men, however changed it may be. Black Annis can feel her power flowing back to her with each meal, the nourishing potency of human children's flesh. Black Annis heaves her burden to her shoulders once again. The delicious smell of fear seeps through the sack. Black Annis breathes it in deeply and tangy saliva floods her mouth as she looks forward eagerly to her next meal . . .

Her luminous eyes can see an opening in the darkness ahead — the entrance to her underground grotto at last. The place is exactly as she left it all those centuries before. But time doesn't matter to Black Annis. She does not age.

She steps through the stone entrance into a large, empty cave. Her eyes glow as she looks around. This still feels like home. She sighs with relief and with weariness. She drops the heap she carries to the ground, and it stirs.

Annis decides she will hold off for a moment. Instead, she unties the fresh pelt from her meal a few hours ago from her skirts and hangs it to dry. Soon there will be another to join it.

She cannot wait any longer.

Black Annis bends low and frees the child she has carried to her lair from the covering that muffles it. In the darkness, at the light first touch of Annis' cold, sharp claws, the child faints, its body going limp. No matter.

She marks the spot she needs with the point of one talon. Then, with one deft movement, she sinks her claw into the child's heart.

Now Black Annis does not hesitate. She makes the first cut in the dead child's skin with her razor-sharp talons. She slices again, deft and sure, and again. In less than a minute, she has another pelt to add to her collection.

Trembling in anticipation of her meal, Black Annis sinks her stained teeth into the flesh, and tears hungrily.

Chapter Five

Callum walked down the hill away from the ruined church with Melissa quietly striding beside him. He could almost feel her brain churning over a fresh argument about being more actively involved in their new mission. He decided it was safer not to talk to her about it for the time being. He had enough on his own mind right now. In any case, they had another task to deal with first . . .

The porch light of Gran's cottage beckoned them back through the cold woodland. Callum could just about make out the figure of his gran in the window, perched on the edge of her armchair in the nook under the stairs, waiting for Callum anxiously. She could see directly up the road out of the sitting room window from that vantage spot, and these days it seemed she was sitting there more and more.

Gran's radio-cassette player was a pretty good indicator of her mood. As Callum opened the front door, he could hear the radio tootling a nervous jazz riff, over and over. But when Callum stepped into the room, the radio gave a burst of static and then went silent. Callum could tell right away that Gran was annoyed with him. It was visible in her thin-lipped, humorless expression.

'That was a very long walk,' Gran said stonily. Then, with a weary effort at politeness, she added, 'Oh, hello, Melissa.'

'Hi, Mrs Scott.'

'I went right up to the edge of the housing estate,' Callum said evasively. 'And then I bumped into Melissa. And, uh, I thought I spotted the cat. I thought maybe he'd strayed off.'

'Cadbury's asleep on the stovetop,' said Gran. 'You know he likes it there when it's still warm. You could have checked. And you could have told me how long you were planning to be out. You know I like to know where you are, especially when it's this late, and especially when . . .'

She let the rest of the sentence go unfinished.

Callum finished it for her. No point in avoiding the issue. 'I know. *Especially when the Shadowing has begun.*'

'It's begun?' Gran repeated anxiously. 'Already? How do you know . . .?'

She trailed off, suddenly glancing at Melissa nervously.

'Don't worry about it,' Callum said curtly. 'Melissa already knows about the Shadowing. Look, Gran, let's just be honest. There's no point in me hiding – I have a duty now.'

'Oh, Callum,' Gran said, unable to keep the concern from her voice. 'You'll do nothing but put yourself in danger. You're a *schoolboy*, for heaven's sake. How do you expect to save the world? It's like . . . it's like a *war*, Callum, and it should be fought by trained soldiers who know what they're doing. You're not strong enough. You don't know enough.'

Callum noticed Melissa was smiling faintly – it was almost the same lecture she'd had from Jacob a quarter of an hour ago. But he wasn't amused.

'Gran,' Callum said. 'The problem is, there are no trained soldiers. I'm the last chime child. This whole thing is falling on *my* shoulders, and I haven't got a clue what's expected of me. If you hadn't kept all of this a secret from me for so long, I'd be a hundred per cent better equipped for dealing with it.'

The accusation stopped Gran in her tracks. She braced herself with her hands gripping the armrests of her chair, her feet flat on the floor. She looked a bit like an old soldier herself, with her short, close-cut iron-grey hair and grim, determined expression.

'Don't be angry, Mrs Scott,' Melissa cut in diplomatically from behind Callum's shoulder. She took a few steps forward and glanced from Gran to Callum, adding earnestly, 'Look, it's bad enough thinking about the Shadowing without us all lying to each other. It's pretty obvious Callum wasn't looking for the cat – he was looking for me. We've had an idea about how to make up for some of that lost time –'

47

'I need my books,' Callum said bluntly.

Gran blinked. 'Your books?'

'The chime child books,' Callum said. 'I need to learn what's in them.'

'Callum, no, you can't just –'

'Gran, I hate to say this, but if you don't hand them over, I'm going to have to just take them.' Callum folded his arms and looked at his grandmother expectantly. Gran matched his gaze for a moment, before finally sighing hard and pushing herself to her feet. She dragged a chair across the room to the high shelf where she had hidden the ancient books behind a bland selection of gardening manuals.

'I don't know how you're going to learn what you need to in the time you've got,' Gran muttered grimly. 'Try the scrapbooks first, maybe . . .'

Callum exhaled and smiled at his gran gratefully.

'Brilliant,' Callum said, but then he hesitated, sure that his next news wouldn't go down well. 'Melissa's actually going to get started with them. We thought – our idea was that Melissa could read the books first, since she already knows a little about what to expect and what she's looking for, and then she could tell me which bits to focus on.'

'But only if it's all right with you, Mrs Scott,' Melissa put in hastily, her gaze as imploring as a puppy's. Callum wanted to tell her that Gran wasn't the sort to be easily won over, but his grandmother was already doing that for him.

'Well, I fail to see how that would work,' Gran said, pausing by the shelf and putting her hands on her hips.

'Uh . . .' Melissa mumbled. 'Well I was hoping to take them home and get reading, so that –'

'Take them home?' Gran said, her voice incredulous. 'Absolutely not.'

'Gran –' Callum began.

'Absolutely not,' Gran said again, her arms folded now. 'Those books do not leave this house.'

Callum set his jaw. He wasn't going to back down – two could play at that game. 'Gran, we have to do this. If Melissa can't take the books home, then she's going to have to come here and read them. Starting tonight.'

He held Gran's gaze for what felt like an eternity

before she finally sighed once more. Climbing on to the chair now by the window, she silently reached up to the top bookshelf behind the low ceiling beam and began to take down the front row of books. Callum let out his breath lightly as she began handing down the first of the ancient books.

'Fine,' Gran said through gritted teeth. She paused. 'Callum, you must know, I'm not doing this willingly. If there was any way I could think of to make sure you didn't have to be involved –'

'Gran . . .' Callum said, shaking his head sadly. Even though he was still angry, he knew this was hard for her. 'I *am* involved. There's no way around it. Look at the mess we got in when you tried to keep me out of it all. Trust me, this is for the best. If Melissa can give me a digested version of what's in the books, it'll leave me more time to try and get up to speed with training to fight . . . whatever it is I'll need to fight.'

Gran pursed her lips. Callum could tell she wanted to say something about his training, but she stopped herself short. 'Well, at the very least, two heads are better than one,' she muttered.

Callum thought the look on her face seemed to suggest she wasn't entirely convinced when it came to Melissa's head.

'Great, thank you, Mrs Scott . . .' Melissa said as she took the books from Gran. Then she paused. Callum could tell from the glint in Melissa's eye that she had some other scheme brewing, but he was shocked by what she said next.

'You know – seeing as I'll be coming here to look at the books anyway, maybe it would help if you would teach me some magic too?'

Gran dropped the book in her hand, startled.

'What? Melissa!' Callum exclaimed.

Melissa rushed over to pick up the book, ignoring both Callum's and his grandmother's surprise, and looking up at the older lady expectantly.

'Callum told me you know some, Mrs Scott, and I just thought –'

'No. *No*. It's much too dangerous,' Gran said to Melissa. 'You may think you've been dabbling in witchcraft with your gothic clothing and your crystals, but believe me, magic is not a game. None of this is.

You have no idea what you're up against.'

'That's my whole point,' Melissa said. '*You* do! Once I start reading these books, I'll start to get an idea too, but I could do more. You've spent the last thirteen years protecting Callum from evil. Think how much stronger your protective spells could be if there were two of us working together!'

'I didn't even let Helen – didn't even ask Callum's own *mother* to share any of this burden with me!' Gran exclaimed. 'You think that if I wouldn't take that risk with my daughter-in-law, I'd ever take such a risk with someone else's child? You don't know me well, but you know me better than that, young lady!'

'Aren't you worried about the idea of Callum facing the Shadowing all alone?' Melissa fired back at her. Callum was impressed at Melissa's perseverance – and her stretching of the truth. 'How can helping me with some magic be more dangerous than that?' Melissa continued. 'What harm can it do to teach me? At least then *I'll* be protected, if nothing else. Make sure Callum's not having to worry about me not being able to handle myself –?'

'What *harm* can it do . . .?' Gran repeated almost to herself, shaking her head. Slowly, she began to stack the gardening manuals back in place, out of habit. The cottage consisted of a small sitting room and kitchen downstairs, and two tiny bedrooms and a bathroom upstairs. Gran kept everything in strict order, including the books.

'I'm not trying to treat you like a child, Melissa,' Gran began again quietly. 'But I just don't believe you understand the risk – how much danger even a small amount of magical knowledge can be, to *yourself* especially.'

She finished stacking the books and climbed down. Callum moved the chair back into its place at the table. In this, at least, he and Gran and even Jacob were united – not one of them thought Melissa should get mixed up in the supernatural any more than was absolutely necessary.

Melissa stood clutching four of the dusty chime child books close to her chest, watching Callum and his grandmother. Her jaw was set determinedly.

'I'll go online.'

It was a threat.

Callum also knew it was something that neither he nor his grandmother could counter or keep a check on. They didn't have a computer. Callum used the internet at school, of course, and at the library – but he didn't have the money to make constant use of Marlock's only cyber café. He wouldn't be able to keep up with Melissa, or to find out what she was doing.

Gran, who Callum was sure knew pretty much zilch about technology, surprised him with her own objection to Melissa's threat.

'The internet is inaccurate and unsafe,' Gran said coolly. 'There's a reason it's called the "web". It lures you in and ties you up. Even if you're researching a straightforward subject, it's sometimes impossible to untangle the misinformation from the real thing, is it not? Try figuring out the history of the radio, or the date of a Shakespeare play, and you could get ten different answers. If it's a risky source for simple historical facts, imagine what it's like for magic. Don't do it.'

Callum looked from his grandmother to Melissa and back again. They were staring at one another unblinkingly.

'Mrs Scott, I don't think you can stop me,' Melissa said carefully.

Gran's jaw clenched. Callum found himself holding back a smile at how Gran's disapproval of his own involvement in the Shadowing had been so quickly overtaken by this new problem.

'Melissa, you can't force this,' he said.

'I know,' she replied. 'It's fine. The internet may not be the best resource, but it's all I've got apparently.'

Callum sighed, exasperated. 'Melissa, you're going to be enough help as it is. Seriously, can't you just –'

'Bring a notebook,' Gran interjected. Both Callum and Melissa turned to look at her, surprised.

'Sorry?' Melissa said.

'Bring a fresh notebook,' Gran repeated. 'Tomorrow after school. And be prepared to listen to absolutely everything I say, without question.'

Melissa gasped. 'Thank you a *million* times!' she exclaimed. 'Look, I know you don't want to do this. I know you don't trust me to do the right thing, and that makes me even *more* grateful. I won't let you down.'

Gran let out a wry, mirthless laugh and shook her head. 'I'm not doing this for you. It's for Callum's protection. I can't have him around someone who's been getting information from goodness knows where, trying to use rogue magic. Your best defence is to learn from a *reliable* source. I have no choice but to do it myself.'

Melissa nodded in silence, then looked down to study the cover of one of the chime child books sheepishly. She cleared her throat. 'OK. Well, if I'm going to be back tomorrow I think I'll wait until then to start reading these too. Uh, thanks again, Mrs Scott.'

Melissa turned to go.

'See you, Callum.'

In spite of himself, Callum couldn't help but return her triumphant grin as he saw her to the door. As he closed it behind Melissa, Callum sighed. After everything that had happened that evening, he felt suddenly exhausted.

'I'm going to bed,' he announced. 'I'll see you in the morning, Gran.'

He started up the narrow spiral stairway.

'Callum, you don't seem bothered by any of this,' Gran said crossly.

'I'm bothered by a lot of things,' Callum said wearily, too tired to argue. He paused. 'Listen, you can trust Melissa, you know. She may be a bit off-the-wall, but she's honest. At least she's not hiding anything.'

'She's determined, I'll give her that,' Gran said, her hands on her hips, ignoring his dig. 'But she's going to have to learn to take the danger seriously. Both of you are. You're up against the *Netherworld*.'

Callum nodded and headed up to his room. But he heard Gran still muttering as he reached the top of the stairs.

'I wish you both knew what you're getting yourselves into . . .'

Chapter Six

In the murky darkness of an abandoned warehouse, a man's footsteps echo across the concrete floor. He is the first to arrive but, as leader, he expected to be. He snaps his fingers. The sound bounces around the corrugated metal walls – and a flickering light appears, dancing at his fingertips. The purple stone of the ring the man always wears reflects the light of the flame. He lowers the small fire to a waiting candlewick, and then goes to light the others. Soon, a circle of light surrounds him. A voice behind him causes him to pause, but as he turns, he smiles.

'Aradia,' he says, greeting the tall, beautiful woman

who has joined him within the circle. Her curtain of red hair glows in the low light.

She stops for a moment, surprised.

'*Varick.*' She nods respectfully, her voice low, velvety. 'So, is it only our Craft names we must use from now on?'

'I think it prudent,' the man replies. 'Where are the others?'

'They follow presently,' Aradia replies. As she speaks, three others file in and their coven is complete. Two men – one thin and lanky with close-cropped, white hair; the other shorter and more youthful, his broad shoulders strong. With them is one other woman. The wrinkles in her dark, worn skin are more exaggerated in the shadowy light, but her violet eyes glint with alertness. Varick eyes the group carefully.

'Brothers and sisters,' he begins, 'the Shadowing falls on our mortal world once more.'

The other coven members nod silently, their faces expectant. They know there is more to come.

'Our master awaits us,' Varick continues. 'For a *century*, he has waited. The Fetch all but completed his mission to eliminate the chime children, as we had summoned him to do. And now, the moment has finally arrived. This time, the Demon Lord will not await the thirteen moons to make his attempt to break through. *This* time, he has our coven on his side. Mortal and Netherworld are united. If our task is successful . . .' He pauses. '*When* we are successful, it will lead to power untold. I trust you are all aware of what we must do?'

'We are,' they chorus.

Varick smiles slowly. 'Very well. Then let us prepare . . .'

Chapter Seven

When the final school bell rang, Callum sprang from his chair and headed to his locker to collect his books. With all that had happened the previous evening, he'd had a terrible night's sleep and an even more distracted day. He was glad to be heading home, even if it would involve a diversion to the churchyard for his next lesson with Jacob and Doom.

The eerie, bitter cold that gripped the country didn't seem to be letting up, and the corridors of Marlock High School were packed with kids muffled in scarves, chattering about the weather. Incredible, Callum thought, how quickly the student population moved on from one issue to the next. A few weeks ago the Fetch had killed Ed Bolton, one of the school's worst bullies, in broad daylight on a public street outside the school – but now everyone seemed caught up in something as mundane as the unnaturally cold weather.

Callum could see Melissa was waiting for him at the gates to the car park. He was pleased she'd waited – they hadn't had a chance to talk properly since everything that happened the night before. Callum was well liked at school, but he had always tried to keep himself apart from other kids – except when he was doing the sports he loved. He hadn't liked the idea of mixing normal people up in his supernatural troubles. But when he'd started talking to Melissa, Callum had realised how much he was missing hanging out with people his own age.

'Hey, Callum.'

As he got closer, Callum almost laughed, but managed to stifle it just in time. Melissa was wearing a scarf made of black wool and glossy green-black feathers, bundled up around her neck so that she looked a bit like a fluffy fledgling blackbird. Melissa might be trustworthy, brave and clever, but she had the most bizarre dress sense of anyone in Marlock High School.

'How mad was last night?' Melissa said, shaking her head. 'And now today seems so normal that it feels like a dream. You know what I mean?'

Callum didn't answer. The events of last night had definitely been stressful, but not really that much weirder than the daily parade of ghosts and premonitions he'd lived with all his life. 'Yeah, it's been a lot to wrap your head around . . .' Callum paused, then blurted, 'Melissa, why did you start going on about wanting Gran to teach you magic?' He knew it was a little abrupt, but he'd been dying to speak to her about it.

'Jacob said only those with power can take on the Netherworld,' Melissa pointed out. 'Lovely Assistant isn't the same thing, is it? I really do want to fight. So I need power. Besides, we need all the help we can get – you're not exactly primed for taking on heaps of Netherworld demons, are you?'

Callum sighed, walking with his head down as usual, trying not to look at the spectres that always haunted the streets of Marlock village. He supposed she had a point.

'What makes you think my *gran's* the source of all knowledge, anyway?' Callum said. 'You saw how she was – she's always on the defensive. All she'll teach you are avoidance tactics. I don't think she knows anything really big, it's all just wards, charms, and little spells and stuff.' He glanced up to look at Melissa. 'But anyway, at least you'll get a chance to crack open the chime child books tonight. Maybe there's something useful in them, something that might even give you a head start, magic-wise.'

'Oh, yeah, definitely!' Melissa's voice was suddenly injected with enthusiasm and excitement. 'I'm really looking forward to going through the books properly. I don't think I've ever actually touched anything so old, you know? And it's really *important*, I'm not just going to be reading them because I'm curious. Plus,' she said with a grin, 'I get to be your teacher, imparting vital chime child knowledge. During our study sessions, you'll be calling me *Miss Roper*, right?'

Callum laughed. 'Dream on!'

They had reached the housing estate at the edge of town. Melissa waved at a couple of little kids messing about on the cable pyramid in the play park.

'Everything seems so *ordinary*, you know?' she said, looking around, her tone serious now.

'Yeah,' Callum agreed. 'And they're all so –'

'– innocent.'

'It scares me,' Callum confessed. 'The way no one knows what's going on. You'd think there ought to be a big media panic: LOCK YOUR DOORS AND STAY AT HOME. THE SHADOWING IS UPON US. But life just seems to be going on like nothing's changed.'

'Well, nothing much has yet,' Melissa said. 'It's like before the Blitz started, isn't it? All the kids had gas masks and got evacuated but nothing happened.'

'At least they were ready. These guys don't have a clue,' Callum muttered. 'And *I'm* the one who's meant to protect them all . . .' He shook his head.

He didn't have a choice; if he had to work twice as

hard, if he had to study twice as much and train for it as well, he'd do it.

'Maybe you should stay for dinner after your lesson with Gran?' Callum said. 'I think we should have our first session as soon as possible.' He needed to prioritise, organise his brain, focus on one skill at a time. That was the kind of thing his rugby coach always encouraged the team to do.

'Yeah,' Melissa replied. 'I'll ring my mum and ask if it's OK.'

Callum nodded, but he was distracted by a strange figure walking along the road some distance ahead of them, near the start of the woods. The man seemed confused and agitated, shuffling back and forth. Something about him seemed odd . . . threatening. Callum's fingertips started to tingle ominously, and a chill swept him as the man slowly turned around. Callum stifled a gasp.

The figure only had half a face.

A gaping, bloody slash was opened across his head from his right temple diagonally down to the left side of his lower jaw – he had no right eye, no nose, no upper lip. Whatever had cleaved the guy's face had mangled half his features. The mutilated man stood staring directly at him. Callum froze. He didn't know what to do – something told him this wasn't a situation he wanted to draw attention to . . .

'Callum,' Melissa's urgent whisper made him jump. 'D'you see that guy up ahead?'

Callum's heart began to beat loudly. 'Uh . . .'

'Just where the footpath goes narrow as it enters the wood,' Melissa said. 'He's got . . . oh, *what*, what's wrong with...' She trailed off, open-mouthed.

'You . . . you can see him?'

The nightmarish figure raised one arm shakily, still staring at Callum with its only eye.

'What do you mean, can I see him? How could I miss him?' Melissa's voice was low and trembling. She took a step backwards. But they both stopped short as the figure opened his mouth.

'Yoooou . . .' His voice was horribly choked.

'Oh, no,' Callum whispered. 'Melissa . . .'

'I-is he talking to you?' she said, her eyes wide.

'Melissa . . .' Callum said again.

'I – Callum, I think he must have escaped from hospital or something . . . I think we should . . .'

'MELISSA!' Callum shouted.

The terrifying figure took a shuffling step towards them.

'Wh-what's he doing?' Melissa's words came out as a strangled murmur.

'Melissa,' Callum croaked. 'That's a *ghost.*'

Chapter Eight

'H-how can it be?' Melissa gasped, frozen to the spot. 'It *can't* be a ghost! I can't see ghosts – except Jacob . . . B-but –'

'RUN!' Callum shouted, grabbing Melissa's arm.

The figure was shuffling towards them with quicker and quicker steps, his ragged clothes floating around him, his arm still outstretched. 'Sssstop . . .' its gurgling voice called after them.

'Callum . . .' Melissa said, her voice tight with panic.

'Over here, behind these trees,' he shouted, ducking behind a frosted trunk deeper into the woods. He and Melissa crouched silently for a moment, watching for movement.

'What does it want?' Melissa whispered, panting.

'I don't know,' Callum said, shaking his head.

'Callum, what on earth is going on?'

'*Shhh*,' Callum said suddenly. 'Don't move.'

The ghost was on the pathway near the trees, like a smudge of dirt and blood across an otherwise pure and glittering landscape. They both stared as it turned its head this way and that: it looked up into the bare, icy canopy above and peered into the woods on either side, then glanced over its shoulder down the road behind it. It was as if the spectre had heard Melissa's cry, and was trying to work out where the noise was coming from.

'Stay still,' Callum hissed. The ghost continued to look around searchingly.

'What do you think he's –?' Melissa began to whisper.

'*Shhh.*' Callum clamped a hand over Melissa's mouth.

But when he looked back at the path, the ghost was gone.

Callum's fingers were beginning to go numb with cold – and the insistent tingling. Turning slowly to see what was there, Callum let out a cry as he saw the bloody face of the ghost loom directly in front of him.

Without thinking, Callum pushed out hard. To his shock, the ghost tumbled backwards. He hadn't made physical contact with the spirit, but the move was enough to confuse it. Before it could recover, Callum leaped from the cover of the trees, grabbing Melissa's arm as he did so.

'Let's get out of here!' he shouted, and together they scrambled back up to the path and ran as fast as they could. They didn't stop until they reached the lane that led to Nether Marlock Church.

'What – what do you think it was going to do?' Melissa gasped, her teeth chattering. She bent over to catch her breath.

'I don't have a clue,' Callum replied, his own breath pluming in rapid clouds in the cold air. 'The ghosts don't usually seem to know what's going on around them. And they've definitely never tried to attack me. Plus I don't understand how *you* could see it too.'

'M-maybe it's part of the Shadowing,' Melissa panted. 'Maybe with more activity around the

Boundary, humans and ghosts are becoming aware of each other.'

Callum nodded. It made some sense, but he certainly didn't like it.

'Well, whatever was going on with him, I think he ought to stay dead,' Melissa said in a low voice, and a visible shiver ran through her whole body. 'Do you think he'll come back?'

Callum clenched his teeth tightly together. 'I doubt it.' He sighed hard. 'I should get to the church, and you should be getting to Gran's.'

'Where shall I tell her you are?'

'Tell her I'm doing some training on my own – she should understand that I need to start . . . preparing. Just don't mention Jacob, obviously.'

Melissa nodded, but she was clearly apprehensive.

'Do you want me to walk with you for a bit?' Callum asked.

Melissa's jaw set. 'No. I'm going to have to start getting used to this sort of thing, I guess.'

Callum nodded, and then tentatively looked around him. The usual ghosts were clustered there at the crossroads, but he found himself eyeing them all closely. Most of them were so familiar to him they now seemed like . . . not old friends, exactly, but at least neutral. They might be hiding dark secrets, but he saw them every day and they minded their own business. There was the figure in the hooded cloak that always stood facing away from Callum. There was the cluster of weeping women in black veils, and there was the gravedigger who had chopped a slice out of his shin with his spade – all milling about in their usual places, and all thankfully ignoring Callum.

'Can you see any ghosts here?' he asked Melissa tentatively.

'No . . .' She stared around her, and then returned her gaze to Callum. 'But they're all around, aren't they? I can sort of *feel* them. You know how it feels when you're in a cinema and it's dark, but you know there are people everywhere?' She hesitated, watching Callum's face closely, and grimaced a little as she spoke. 'I'm right, aren't I?'

Callum nodded grudgingly. He didn't want to scare her, but as he looked around him again he realised the ghosts were looking at each other anxiously, as though they were suspicious of one another. One of the veiled women kept glancing over her shoulder at the gravedigger; the gravedigger kept waving his spade threateningly at the cloaked figure. Their movements were nervous and furtive. They seemed confused and – was it possible for a ghost to be afraid?

Maybe not afraid. But certainly uneasy. Still, they seemed oblivious to Callum and Melissa, for now at least.

'It's the usual suspects though,' Callum said. 'I know it's a bit creepy, but I don't think you'll run into any trouble.'

Melissa gave him a wry smile. 'Let's hope not. Remember the good old days when the only thing to worry about was the Fetch digging my eyes out of my head?'

Callum laughed. 'Sure you'll be OK?'

'I'll be fine.' She gave a quick wave, took a deep breath and then set off down the road towards Gran's cottage. Callum watched until she was out of sight, and then he turned towards Church Lane.

*

As Callum let himself through the gate, the evening was already drawing in and the churchyard was in shadow. Jacob and Doom were waiting for him in their usual spot beneath the yew at the far end of the cemetery. Jacob tilted his head slightly in greeting and, without a sound, Doom stalked to Callum's side to lead him into the ruined church.

'Something really strange happened on the way here,' Callum told Jacob. 'There was a ghost on the Nether Marlock Road, a new one I've never seen – and Melissa could see it too.'

Jacob frowned. 'Has she seen shades before?'

'Only you. She thought it might be to do with the movements around the Boundary – a sign of the Shadowing.'

'She is likely correct. There will be more of this as each moon progresses – growing numbers of the living people in your world will be able to see the spirits.

Many of them will, of course, refuse to believe what their eyes tell them.'

'Well, there was no avoiding this one. It tried to *attack* us. It was weird, like he'd suddenly become aware of everything around him.'

Jacob paused.

'Yes. With some of the shades, when the Shadowing comes, they become more aware of themselves, and their . . . circumstances. How they came to be as they are. They become restless.'

'Do you think that ghost will give us trouble again?' Callum asked, frowning with concern. He wished he had a mobile so he could check Melissa made it to Gran's OK.

'I think not. Most of them will be transients. I am certain the spirit you saw will have already moved on.'

Callum nodded. 'Good.'

Jacob paced away from Callum then turned, and clasped his blood-stained fingers together. 'Are you ready?'

'To see more ghosts?'

A faint smile crossed Jacob's gleaming white features.

'I meant, ready for the lesson. The reason you are here.'

'You don't take any prisoners, do you?' Callum said. 'Come on then.'

Jacob gave an almost imperceptible nod, and Doom bounded at Callum.

It was like going right back to the beginning. What little Callum had learned last night, he seemed to have completely forgotten now. Doom bowled him over in a single leap. The spectral dog didn't even bother to hold Callum down this time, just strode away.

'Humph,' was all Jacob said.

Jacob's indifference made Callum even more irritated with himself. He got to his feet determinedly.

You've got to master this, he thought. *You don't have any choice. You just fought off that ghost, you can do this . . .*

'Why don't *you* try it,' Callum challenged Jacob.

'What do you mean?'

'Attack me. Do it yourself.'

'I see no point. You are not afraid of me. It is *fear* you are learning to battle against. Once you have done that, you will be able to focus and concentrate your abilities.'

'I'm definitely a little afraid of you,' Callum confessed. 'You're not exactly cuddly, you know. And if I can get the hang of putting up a barrier against *you*, maybe I can make a stronger one next time, and it'll work against Doom as well.'

Jacob nodded silently, but before Callum could say anything more, the Born Dead faded from view entirely. Callum was left with only Doom, who stared at him with huge red eyes.

'Jacob?' Callum's voice sank into the growing darkness. He swung around, scouring the corners of the ruined church, but Jacob had disappeared. Callum jumped as Doom began to emit a low, warning growl.

'Jacob?'

Silence, except for Callum's own ragged breathing. 'This isn't funny. Jacob?'

'Behind you.'

The whisper was in Callum's ear, close and sudden. Callum whirled but, behind him, instead of Jacob in his normal form, his body was stretched to twice its usual height. Black blood leaked from his eyes and ears and dripped from his fingertips, which had become elongated and claw-like. With a terrifying shriek, the ghost hurled himself at Callum.

Chapter Nine

'NO!' Callum shouted, throwing his hands out protectively. He braced himself for impact, but instead of connecting, he felt Jacob pushing against some invisible barrier, before stumbling back from him. Callum watched in relief as the Born Dead shrank back to his normal size in front of his eyes.

'Blimey,' Callum breathed. 'This is definitely a better look for you. I mean, that was . . . I didn't even know you could *do* that.' He attempted a smile, but he could feel the palms of his hands tingling – the feeling was running up his arms. He folded them and looked over at Jacob. But the ghost looked surprised.

'You did it.'

Callum frowned in confusion, but then it dawned on him. 'You mean the shield thing? The chime child shield?'

'Yes, Callum, you *blocked* me,' Jacob said.

Callum grinned at him. 'I suppose I did.'

Jacob nodded approvingly. 'You controlled your fear, and you focused. Well done.'

Callum smile faded a little – he hadn't really tried to do it deliberately.

'How did you feel?' Jacob asked. 'Think it through.'

'Well, I *was* afraid but I . . .' Callum paused, running it back through his mind. 'I suppose I just went on instinct, and I was just thinking about the irony. You know, second ghost attack in as many hours. And I sort of knew what you were doing was an illusion. At least, I *assume* it was illusion?'

Jacob nodded, with a hint of a smile. 'It was.'

'So maybe it was a bit different from how I feel about Doom. I *know* what Doom can do with those teeth. He tore the Fetch to ribbons.' Callum gave a weak laugh, but Jacob was still nodding.

'It does not matter what your reason was. You did it. You are making progress.'

Callum raised his eyebrows. 'Yeah. I suppose so.' He still wasn't sure, though. What use was it if he could only use his powers by accident?

'Try again,' Jacob said. 'Try again with Doom. Only this time, remember how you felt when I attacked – singularly focused on stopping the blow.'

Callum nodded and took a deep breath.

'Doom.'

Doom leaped, but as soon as he did, Callum panicked and the dog slammed into him. Callum collapsed to the ground, and Jacob shook his head.

But another 45 minutes later, Callum still hadn't got anywhere. Jacob was relentless.

'Again.'

'Wait,' Callum said tightly. He clenched his jaw, his frustration causing prickling heat to rise up his neck despite the pressure from Dooms icy paws. The Grim released him, but Callum stayed on the ground. He sat up, his hands bunched in fists on his knees. 'This isn't working. Maybe . . . I don't know, maybe if you both attacked at the same time?'

Jacob's sunken black eyes held a faint gleam of amusement. 'You mean maybe your distrust of me will help you defend yourself against the Grim?'

Callum ignored him. 'I just . . . I need the most extreme challenge I can get. This is too slow . . . I'm not going to get anywhere at this rate. I need to be able to deal with bigger stuff, sooner.'

Jacob looked at Callum for a minute, as though assessing how serious he was. Then he held out his pale hand to pull Callum up. His dead skin was cold as the frosted stone of the church walls.

'Both of us at once,' Jacob said.

Callum nodded seriously, and braced himself.

Doom leaped towards Callum's throat with his icy fangs bared; Jacob transformed into the hideous image of himself once again, lashing out ferociously with bloody claws.

'BACK!' Callum shouted at once, squeezing his eyes shut and waiting for impact.

Stay back. Callum fixed the thought in his mind – and to his amazement, as he opened his eyes again, he saw that Jacob and Doom were pushing against a shimmering barrier. They couldn't touch him. Callum felt focused. He was doing it! He was actually –

But it only worked for a moment. As soon as he began to congratulate himself, the barrier collapsed. Doom snarled viciously, his teeth scraping dangerously close to Callum's skin as Jacob tackled him around the waist. Callum slammed to the ground hard.

How was he *still* not getting this? Callum squeezed his eyes closed and let out a fierce cry of frustration that echoed into the gathering night.

'Get up. We will try it again.' Callum opened his eyes as he heard Jacob's voice. The Born Dead was looming over him with a faint smile.

*

An hour later and darkness had fallen, but the welcoming light was on over the cottage porch. Callum stood for a moment with his hand on the latch, trying to shake off the halting progress of his training session, and bracing himself for more tension inside the cottage. But when he let himself in, he was amazed at the sight that greeted him.

Gran and Melissa were both sitting at the table, with Gran's old radio-cassette player in front of them. The chime child books and various discarded sheets of paper lay on the floor around. Melissa was grinning broadly, and even Gran had the beginnings of a smile playing on her lips.

'Try it again –' Gran looked up. '– Oh, hello, Callum.'

'Callum!' Melissa exclaimed. 'Come and see what I've been learning!' She tucked her wild, curly hair behind her ears, eyes shining with excitement. 'Watch,' she said, but then hesitated. 'Actually, can you show me one more time, Mrs Scott?'

'Frank Sinatra,' Gran commanded her radio, one hand hovering in the air above it.

On cue, a jaunty crooning started up. Gran hadn't touched the radio.

Melissa leaned close to it, bringing both palms above the old radio. 'OK, here we go.' She took a deep breath. 'Um . . . Nine Inch Nails!'

The radio instantly changed tunes, and thundering

heavy rock began to blare out of its speaker instead.

'Louder!' Melissa told it.

The volume increased and the table began to rattle with the noise.

'Whoa,' Melissa exclaimed as the music became deafening. She narrowed her eyes, and the song swelled to a dramatic close.

Melissa leaned back for a minute looking triumphant. Gran nodded once and gave Melissa a tight smile. 'That's it.'

Callum was impressed, and not just with the magic. If it wasn't quite hugs all round between Gran and Melissa, it was certainly going better than he'd expected it to.

'Cool,' Callum said, though he couldn't help feeling a bit subdued. Why was it Melissa could get the hang of things so quickly when he'd been struggling all evening to do something that was supposed to come naturally? He sighed. 'So it's going well then?'

'Melissa's a fast learner,' Gran said. She glanced over at Melissa's grinning face. 'Of course, you have to remember that this isn't too difficult, manipulating something as simple as this old radio's mechanism . . .'

'We've been working on a few other things as well,' Melissa told Callum eagerly, oblivious to Gran's cautions. 'And before you ask, don't worry – I've made a start on reading the chime child books too.'

Callum smiled weakly. Of course she'd managed to fit that in too. He folded his arms and tried not to think about how far he still had to go.

'How . . . uh, how was your practice?' Gran asked, interrupting his thoughts. 'Are you sure it's a good idea trying to work on your skills by yourself?'

Callum glanced at Melissa, but she nodded encouragingly.

'It was fine,' Callum said quickly. 'A bit of a struggle I guess, but once Melissa and I start going through the books it will get better.'

'Are you sure you don't want me to help you though, Callum? I could –'

'Gran, I think it's better if you focus on helping Melissa. It's stuff you know more about. You're not a chime child; I don't think you can help me with this. I'm going to work on it myself,' Callum said, with what he hoped was an air of finality. He didn't want Gran asking too many questions.

'Right,' Gran said curtly, though a hint of worry creased her brow. 'If you say so.'

Callum bristled, though he knew she was right to be sceptical.

'Anyway, didn't you say you had something on tonight? I thought Melissa and I might have some time for her to start telling me about the chime child books.'

'Well I'm glad you have my diary in check,' Gran said lightly, but Callum could hear the irritation in her voice. 'One of my old pupils has an art show on at the village hall.' She started up the narrow staircase, moving deliberately slowly as she made her way to her little bedroom.

Callum exhaled. The tense atmosphere between him and his gran was starting to get to him. It was times like this that he missed his mum more than ever. She always kept the peace, and she always knew exactly what to say to make him feel better. He shook his head and turned to Melissa.

'That went well,' he said with a wry smile.

'She'll come round. Anyway, listen, I spoke to Mum and she's fine with me staying for dinner. Obviously I didn't mention the tomes of ancient lore that we'll be studying . . . I may have substituted that for maths.'

Callum laughed. It felt good to be in the warm with a friend after the troublesome evening he had had so far.

'OK then. How about a bit of pasta?'

'Sounds good,' Melissa said, though her face fell as Callum stepped over to the kitchen and pulled a can of spaghetti hoops out of the cupboard. After heating it up on the stove, Callum brought two bowls over just as Gran came downstairs and put on her coat. Callum felt a twinge of worry.

'You'll be careful walking to the village, won't you, Gran?'

She tutted at him, but Callum could tell his gran was pleased that he was concerned.

'I'll be fine. Don't make a mess,' she said, eyeing Melissa in particular. 'I'll be back in an hour or so. And for heaven's sake, try not to get into any trouble.'

'No trouble? Too late,' Callum muttered as Gran closed the door behind her.

He turned to Melissa and couldn't help chuckling at the smattering of spaghetti hoops already spread across the table. 'Right then, do you want to impart some of your new chime child wisdom, O Teacher?'

Melissa grinned and rolled her eyes. She took a deep breath, then her words tumbled out in an excited rush.

'Well, these four books I've looked at so far are a pretty good selection of what's there, I think. One of them is like that printed encyclopaedia we had a quick look at before the whole Fetch thing. Callum, it's *ancient* – I think it dates to 1535 or something. Thank goodness it's printed, I'd never be able to read it if it was handwritten. I mean, it makes your eyes cross as it is – really weird letters. And the woodblock pictures, they're *amazing*. You look at the picture and you don't see anything at first, then you start to pick out all these odd details –' She paused to draw another sharp breath. 'And then you sort of wish you hadn't looked so close, because it's a picture of an old woman chewing on a kid's arm like it's a chicken drumstick, or something, and then you can't get it out of your head. Wow, I kind of wish I hadn't brought it up while I was eating . . .'

Callum laughed at her description – he couldn't help it.

'It's not funny!' Melissa protested.

'No, I know . . . but the way you tell it is.'

Melissa punched him lightly on the arm.

'Ow! OK, OK, so what are the other books like?' Callum said.

'They're all handwritten – diaries and journals kept by other chime children – your predecessors, I suppose. One of the diaries is about 150 years old and the handwriting is really beautiful, so I had a good look at that one because it was the easiest to read. It's actually a copy of an earlier diary, but it's not pleasant reading. I don't think any of them are. Terrifying stories about battles with demons but also some useful notes on their powers and weaknesses, stuff I've never heard of at *all*. Mostly the chime children don't seem to have relied on targeting a demon's weak point to defeat it. They made the most of their own powers and *that's* what won the battle. Callum, it's amazing what chime children seem to be able to do! Like, did you know you can control animals? How cool is that? Hey . . . Callum, are you listening?'

It would be a lot easier to concentrate, Callum thought, *if my hands weren't so cold*. Despite having been inside for a while, his hands were tingling so hard they actually *hurt*.

Tingling . . .?

Suddenly, Callum's focus was shattered. His brain felt as though it had been pierced by a searing hot knife. He fell backwards out of his chair and on to the floor. His eyes were open, but he saw nothing. Nothing but complete blackness. The utter, darkness of being underground . . .

*

Callum's eyes slowly adjusted to the darkness around him. He was having some sort of vision, but it felt different to any he'd had before. It felt as though he was moving around someone else's dream, and somehow he instinctively knew that it wasn't happening now, or even any time in the immediate future. It was almost like . . . a premonition. He took a deep breath.

A pair of glowing eyes began to emerge from the blackness. The eyes blinked, causing light to fade in and out of the dark space eerily. Callum could hear a strange clattering, which he realised was coming from the figure with the glowing eyes. Was that noise being made by its teeth? He couldn't make out any more of its features in the gloom, but he jumped as he heard a man's voice somewhere behind him in the darkness, beginning to chant in a language he couldn't understand.

Before Callum's eyes, murky shadows began to emerge from the darkness, illuminated by what he soon realised was a glowing ring on the chanting man's hand. As his voice grew louder, Callum realised that there were other people in the shadows, joining the man in his chants. They were standing in a circle around the figure with the glowing eyes. Then the man with the ring raised his arms aloft and the sound from the group grew faster and more insistent. Callum could make out the strange creature with the glowing eyes more clearly as the half-light of the man's ring shone brighter.

It was a woman – of sorts.

The chanting group was encircling a blue-skinned, tall, thin . . . hag. Her skin looked ancient and papery, with the unnatural, deathly hue of a cadaver. Her long straggly hair hung around a demonic face punctured by a mouthful of black, pointed teeth. Callum was right – it was those teeth that clattered with a sound like marbles spilling on to a concrete floor. But the most disturbing sight of all was the woman's hands – and her talon-like fingernails. Impossibly long, the claws bent and curled horribly, hanging down at her sides.

Then the woman began to turn, slowly at first, as though she was trying to resist the movement. The five people surrounding her stretched their arms out towards her, their palms held upwards, their chanting reaching a crescendo. The hag began to spin faster and faster and faster, until she became a blur of blue skin and gnarled talons, her clattering teeth creating a deathly din.

Callum gasped. He realised with horror that the hag's own arms were now outstretched – and the claws in her fingers were being pulled *right out of her*. A deafening scream pierced through all the other noise as the twisted talons were ripped from her fingers in a shower of blue-black blood.

Then there was a blast of scorching heat, and the scene began to glow with a terrifying, overwhelming crimson light . . .

Chapter Ten

With a jolt, Callum came to. He was lying flat on his back in the living room, among the chime child books and bits of paper his gran and Melissa had scattered on the floor. His spaghetti hoops lay in a heap next to him, the bowl upturned.

'So much for keeping things tidy, eh?' he croaked.

Melissa knelt by him, her face a picture of concern. One of her hands hovered uncertainly in the air above Callum's shoulder, as though she thought it might help to touch him but didn't quite dare.

'Are you awake?' Melissa said. 'Are you all right?'

Callum sat up and rubbed his eyes hard, trying

to clear his head. 'Yeah,' he mumbled. 'I'm OK.'

'Was it a vision?'

He drew in a sharp breath and nodded. 'What exactly did you see?' Melissa pressed. 'It really knocked you for six – I thought you might have fainted for a second there. I've never seen you react to one like that before.'

'It was like – it was like being hit over the head with a hot poker,' Callum said. 'It felt strange, surreal – like it was stronger than any I've had before, reaching further into the future or something.' His words came out in a stutter. 'I-it was . . . I saw a group of people. Humans, I'm almost certain. But there was one other there who . . . wasn't. The humans, five of them, were all circled around this woman, this *hag*. She had blue skin and claws – her claws were insanely long and sharp. They were doing some kind of ritual, I think.' Callum shook his head, trying to clear the terrifying image from his mind.

'Humans performing a ritual on something from the Netherworld?' Melissa said. 'That sounds bad. Really bad. You don't think it's the same people who brought the Fetch over?'

Callum swallowed, and Melissa stood up and helped him to his feet. His mouth felt dry. He took a big gulp of water from a glass on the table.

'It would make sense, wouldn't it,' he said. 'Although it looked like this time they might have something more in mind than using a Netherworld demon as an assassin . . .'

'What do you mean?' Melissa asked.

'Well . . . I think they were sacrificing the hag.'

Melissa's eyes widened. 'Sacrificing? Well, we have to do something.'

Callum raised his eyebrows. 'Like what? I have no idea where that was . . . or *when* exactly it will be, even.' He sighed in frustration – but then an idea hit him. 'Hang on. There's at least one thing we can do – we can look this hag woman up, see if the chime child books say anything about her.'

'Good idea,' Melissa said, clearly pleased to have something to focus on. Callum tidied up the sitting room while she began to flick carefully through the pages of one of the books.

'Ugh,' Melissa groaned, holding the book up to

show Callum a graphically detailed image of a two-headed beast with blood oozing from its mouth and eyes. 'Here's hoping *that's* not heading our way any time soon.'

Callum nodded grimly and Melissa turned the page quickly.

'Oh!' she exclaimed suddenly.

'What is it?' Callum asked, sitting down beside her to look at the page she was staring at. It was the picture Melissa had mentioned earlier – a woman gnawing a child's arm . . .

'Oh,' Callum echoed, swallowing hard. He read the inscription below the picture aloud. 'Black Annis . . . child-eating crone.'

Melissa nodded. 'I should have recognised your description – blue skin, impossibly long claws, pointed teeth . . . Callum, do you think Black Annis might have crossed over from the Netherworld already?'

'It's possible,' Callum muttered, though he hoped he was wrong. 'She eats *children*?'

'That's what it says,' Melissa replied. She paused for a moment, reading more. 'This demon yearns uncontrollably for their flesh . . . and she has magical abilities, but the notes here say they are "base and lacking in subtlety". Oh, wait . . . this might be useful. It says here that Black Annis used to lurk in the hills around what is now Leicester.'

Callum looked at Melissa – her eager gaze told him she was thinking the same thing he was. 'Tomorrow's a teacher training day, right?' he began.

'Yeah,' Melissa replied eagerly.

'So maybe we could get the train to Leicester and just check things out . . . see if we can find any clues on what those humans might have planned? At least it would be a starting point.'

'Yeah, sure,' Melissa said. 'Do you think your gran would be OK with that though?'

Callum shook his head. 'I'll just tell her we're going into Manchester for the day – she doesn't need to know where we're really going.'

Melissa grinned, and then began gathering her stuff into her enormous, mirror-covered black bag. 'OK. Let's get the early train then. I'll meet you at the station, nine o'clock sharp.'

'Cool,' Callum said.

'Listen, I'd better get going,' Melissa said, but she hesitated as she reached the door. 'Callum . . . this is just the start, isn't it?'

Callum was quiet for a moment. 'Yeah . . . yeah, I think it is.'

They looked at one another silently. It didn't really bear thinking about what could be out there, or what they might be getting themselves into.

'I'll see you tomorrow,' Callum said. 'You'll be all right getting home?'

'Yep,' Melissa said, taking a deep breath and pulling her coat closer around her. Callum gave his friend a reassuring smile as he shut the door behind her.

Turning back into the cottage, Callum took a deep breath and closed his eyes for a moment, enjoying the quiet. He felt exhausted, and he knew Melissa was right the worst hadn't even begun. He felt like he was battling against a raging tide, with no idea what was out there – it all felt so out of his control.

But control seemed to be the key to it all: controlling his excuses to Gran; controlling his fears so he could create a shield against evil; controlling his chime child visions. The powers were all there, but at the moment they seemed to be almost completely *outside* of his control. Callum let out another grunt and clenched his fists, taking the opportunity to vent his frustration while he was alone.

But as he unfurled them, Callum looked down at his hands. It was true – the powers were all there, literally in his hands. He remembered how his mum always used to say, 'Attitude is a little thing that makes a big difference.' That's why she was so into her climbing; the idea of tackling something that seemed insurmountable. The thought boosted Callum. He *could* do this. He'd fought off that crazy ghost after all, right? He had it in him; he just had to try even harder, learn to use his powers at will, to get as good as he possibly could.

Maybe it was easier said than done. But he had to try . . .

Suddenly, a new thought made Callum's muscles tense. That ghost in Marlock Wood had spoken to him, had known Callum was there. What if . . . Callum was almost afraid to think it, but what if the Shadowing had one positive outcome?

If ghosts were able to see mortals, then maybe, just maybe, he could find and actually speak to the ghost of his mother?

It would make everything worthwhile. Callum had never felt so determined. *I'll do whatever it takes*, he swore to himself. *Whatever it takes.*

Chapter Eleven

Melissa came pelting down the platform the next morning minutes before the train to Leicester pulled into Marlock station.

'Whoa! Slow down,' Callum said with a grin. 'What happened to nine o'clock sharp?'

'Ha ha,' Melissa retorted. 'Have you seen this?'

She thrust a newspaper into his hands, and Callum's face fell. SECOND CHILD MISSING FROM LEICESTER SUBURB, the headline shouted.

'Two kids, vanished. The first one was a nine-year-old boy – just completely vanished from his *bedroom* at some point during the night. I saw his mum being interviewed on the telly this morning – it was awful, the poor lady was really distraught. The police are searching a wood nearby.' Melissa shook her head. 'I don't think it's a coincidence, do you?'

Callum's heart sank. No, it probably couldn't be a coincidence. The train pulled in, and they both took their seats in silence.

'Maybe this is a mistake,' Melissa said in a low voice. 'I mean, if Black Annis is already running around snatching children, it could be dangerous us going to Leicester at all.'

Callum shook his head. 'We just need to check things out, see if we can get any clues – especially what those humans want with her. We're going to be careful, don't worry.'

Melissa nodded, but they both sat the rest of the journey in preoccupied silence. Fields and houses flashed past outside, and Callum watched them go by with a growing sense of unease. He didn't want to admit it, but a tingling feeling was building in his hands as the train rattled along. Something was wrong, he just didn't know what.

He was almost surprised when the train came to a stop and he saw the sign for Leicester hanging over the platform.

'Come on,' Melissa said, gathering her coat. As they disembarked, Callum felt his hands tingling more and more furiously. He knew he should tell Melissa that something was up, but as he opened his mouth to speak he was interrupted by the whoop of a police siren.

'What's going on?' Melissa said. They walked quickly out of the ticket hall to the front of the station, where a crowd was gathering. One police car was already parked in the forecourt and another was pulling up to the pavement beneath a jaunty sign announcing 'Welcome to Leicester!'

In contrast to the sign's cheerful message, nearby stood a sobbing woman with three police officers gathered round her – one asking questions, one taking notes, and another radioing out an alert.

'. . . She was just with me . . . sh-she was right next to me . . .' the woman was saying between sobs. 'I stopped to use the ticket machine outside the station and when I turned around she was . . . she was just *gone* . . .' Her shoulders began to shake, and then she stopped and sniffed hard. One of the officers stepped in.

'What does your daughter look like, madam?'

'She's just a girl, she's only eight-and-a-half years old . . . please!'

'Can you describe her for us?'

'Sh-she has long blonde hair – it's almost white – and blue eyes. Big blue eyes. Her name's Rachael! Please, you have to find her . . .' The woman's tears overwhelmed her, and one of the officers put an arm around her.

'Oh no!' Melissa said, turning to Callum. 'Do you think it's . . .'

Callum nodded, but he couldn't speak. He could feel the maddening buzzing in his hands, and he knew that a vision was about to hit him. He reached out to a wall to steady himself and tried to open himself up to the image.

It was quick, but it was enough to set his head spinning. He had a flashing vision of a hag-like woman dragging a blonde-haired girl into an alleyway and then throwing off her hood. Callum blinked as the vision faded, and swallowed hard. He was almost certain the woman was the same one he'd seen in his previous vision – and he was also certain that it was the girl the woman had just described.

'Melissa, we have to go NOW!' he hissed, his heart racing with panic.

'What did you see?'

'Black Annis – she was dragging the girl away. I think they must be somewhere nearby; she can't have got far on foot. Come on, we might still have time.' Callum pushed desperately through the small crowd and out on to the road. Melissa ran behind him, trying to keep up. She stumbled backwards as a car sped out in front of them.

'Callum, wait!' she shouted. 'We don't even know where we're going!'

Callum slowed down, panting. 'I saw an alleyway, next to a café.'

'OK, just think!' Melissa said as she caught up to

him. 'We need to find out exactly where it is. Did you see what the café was called?'

'Sunrise . . . The Sunrise Café,' Callum said, then reached out and grabbed a passing man's arm. 'Excuse me, sir. Can you tell me where the Sunrise Café is?'

The man eyed Callum suspiciously for a moment, then answered, 'Next road along, on the left.'

Callum and Melissa broke into a sprint. Callum could see the café up ahead, and the relentless tingling in his hands ramped up again. He rounded the corner into the alleyway, but then skidded to a halt. He was totally unprepared for what he saw.

The alley was a dead end. Hunched against the brick wall at the far end was a woman dressed in ragged clothes, her hair clumped like thick ropes, hiding her face.

Her clawed hands were holding something . . . someone.

Callum retched.

The crone was pressing something up to her mouth. Something bloody, fleshy, but devoid of skin.

A body. A corpse.

The only thing recognisably human about it was a cascade of long, white-blonde hair, caked with blood.

'N . . . no . . .' Callum's voice strangled in his throat.

Then he heard Melissa's scream.

Chapter Twelve

Callum barely even had time to think. With a furious yell, he ran towards Black Annis, his hands raised in front of him. Shock and anger made his entire body quiver, and he felt a surge of energy pressing out from his hands. This was no warning – *it was power.*

Black Annis dropped the corpse and leaped at Callum. Her black, pointed teeth were bared and dripping with the girl's blood. But as she pounced, Callum felt the energy in his hands push out and surround him. The hag twisted mid-leap and was knocked sideways. She landed in a crouch, shaking her head from side to side. For a moment, Black Annis looked confused, but then a dawning realisation spread across her face.

'*Chime child* . . .' she hissed, her voice a hideous rasp.

'Callum, run!' Melissa shouted, and Callum whirled around to her – he'd almost forgotten she was there.

'No, Melissa, you get out of here. I'm –'

'LOOK OUT!' Melissa screamed, and Callum turned just in time to see Black Annis leaping towards him once more, her talons flexed and pointed straight at him. He threw his hands up in front of him, and Annis was knocked backwards again by his shield. But this time she recovered quickly. The demon snarled and lashed out – Callum only just managed to jump out of the way in time.

But Annis' attentions had shifted. Callum followed the crone's glowing gaze and saw it fall on Melissa, who was standing at the open end of the alleyway, her eyes wide with shock. In a split second, Black Annis sprang right over his head towards Melissa.

'MELISSA!' Callum shouted, but it was too late. He saw his friend hit the ground hard. Black Annis pinned her down and then she bared her teeth, the horrible slash of black in blue skin, and sank them into Melissa's shoulder. She cried out in agony.

'NO!' Callum didn't even use his powers this time. With a roar, he launched himself in a rugby tackle at the hag, knocking her off Melissa. Desperately trying to avoid the witch's flailing talons, he pulled at her hair as hard as he could, grimacing as a stringy clump came away in his hand. Annis gave a screech and jerked away from him, retreating into the alleyway.

Rage filled Callum as he regained his footing and stood between Melissa and the hag. Black Annis ran towards the wall at the far end of the alley and began scrabbling up the brickwork with her impossibly long talons.

Callum raised his hands and reached towards her with a wordless cry of anger and loathing.

The palm of his hand suddenly crackled with energy. He felt the force radiating from deep within him and out through his hands as raw power. A glowing ball of light flickered in his palms, rippling in waves like heat from a bonfire.

Callum aimed towards Black Annis and released the bolt of energy at her. The crackling ray hit her arm and she screamed in pain once again. One of her clawed hands lost its grip, but she'd already reached the top of the wall. She pulled herself up, but a row of barbed wire blocked her way. She paused. Seizing the moment, Callum re-directed the beam of energy that was still radiating from his outstretched hand back towards the crone. He missed, but the energy struck the taut, spiked wire, which broke and sprang free, whipping out across the hag's face. Thick, blue-black blood oozed from the wound, and Black Annis let out a high-pitched, bloodcurdling scream. Then she hauled herself over the wall through the gap that had been created and disappeared out of sight.

Callum stared at his outstretched hand, stunned. The air around it still crackled with power.

'What the . . .?' he breathed.

Then, through the shimmering air, Callum saw Melissa, still lying in agony on the ground at the entrance to the alleyway.

He rushed to her side. Her wrist was bleeding badly

– she'd managed to cross her arm over her neck when the monster had attacked her, and it was her wrist that had been savaged by the hag's pointed teeth, not her shoulder. Blood soaked her sleeve and mitten. Her face was drained white as chalk. She looked down at her hand and gave a grunt of distress.

'Are you OK?' Callum gasped. 'Did she get you anywhere else? Let's get out to the street, we should take you to a hospital –'

He clasped above her injured wrist gently, hoping to stem the bleeding, his own hands still tingling with residual energy.

'Callum!' Melissa gasped, more in surprise than pain. 'Wh-what are you doing?'

Callum looked at her, confused, but Melissa was staring down at her wrist. Tentatively, she lifted back her blood-soaked sleeve and stared down at the wound. Where Callum held her, prickling energy flowed over and around both their hands. Callum could feel the electric warmth radiate from his palms. The power wasn't as strong as it had been, but the air was still rippling. The force flowed around the gaping slashes in Melissa's wrist – which slowly, before their eyes, began to seal themselves closed. After a few moments, the ripples stopped and Callum took his hand away.

'What *was* that?' Melissa asked. The strength had come back into her voice.

'I'm not sure . . .' Callum didn't know what to tell her. 'I – I think it's done something though . . .'

He broke off into silence and they both stared down at her arm again in amazement. Where the savage teeth had torn the flesh, it was now smooth and unbroken. The fading energy of Callum's power had somehow repaired the damaged skin without even leaving a scar.

'Wow,' Melissa breathed, then paused for a moment and stared at Callum. 'You *healed* it! That's another one of your powers! And Callum, what you did with that beam of energy. That was amazing! You're really starting to get the hang of this.' Her voice was shaking and incredulous.

Callum swallowed hard and looked down the alleyway at the crumpled corpse of the blonde-haired girl. His stomach turned over and he had to look away.

'Fat lot of difference it made,' he muttered, and then turned to look at Melissa, whose face was serious again.

'Maybe we should go and tell those police officers . . .'

Callum frowned and took a deep breath.

'We can't. I mean, if we go to the police, they'll ask questions, you have blood on your sleeve . . .' He trailed off, shaking his head. His stomach was in knots. Melissa nodded.

'You're right. Someone will find her soon enough,' she said, her eyes glazing over. Callum squeezed her shoulder briefly.

'Let's get out of here.'

Chapter Thirteen

'Don't you just want to get home?' Melissa asked as Callum walked her to her front door from Marlock station.

He shook his head grimly. 'I've got to go to the churchyard. I want to know what the hell all that was. Maybe Jacob can shed some light on it.'

Melissa sighed. 'I'd come with you, but I know my parents are going to be wondering where I am by now. Listen, thanks for everything today. I'm just sorry that we . . .' She trailed off, her eyes welling up at the memory. A tear spilled over and she wiped it away quickly. 'I'm sorry we didn't get there in time.'

Callum watched as she went inside, then set off at a determined pace for the churchyard. Jacob and Doom were waiting beneath the yew tree. Jacob's pale skin seemed to glisten a little in the dusky light of the afternoon.

'Callum,' Jacob said as he strode over. 'I did not expect you for some hours yet.'

Callum quickly explained what had happened in Leicester, the ghost listening intently with his arms folded. When Callum finished, Jacob shook his head, his pale brow furrowed.

'Black Annis? How did you even know she had crossed over?'

Callum sighed – he hadn't mentioned his initial vision.

'I . . . I saw something – it was like a premonition almost. It wasn't clear at first, everything was in darkness and shadows, but there was a group of humans, and they seemed to be performing a ritual . . . a sacrifice maybe, on this hag-like demon. Then Melissa looked up the thing I described, and it was obvious it was Black Annis.'

Jacob's face was grim. 'It would seem that your visions are becoming more prescient with the onset of the Shadowing. That you are seeing further into the future. This is to be expected.' He paused. 'Start from the beginning. Tell me everything you saw.'

When Callum explained his vision in more detail, Jacob seemed even more unhappy. He paced away from Callum and kept his back turned. Doom followed, as though awaiting some instruction. Finally Jacob turned and spoke, fixing Callum with a hard stare.

'Callum, I do not think I need to tell you how severe this situation is. Firstly, you should not have gone off in the hope of attacking a Netherworld being about which you knew nothing.'

'Hang on,' Callum interjected. 'That's not true, we *did* know something about her, and that's why we were so anxious to find out more. We were looking for clues. And once we ran into her, I had no choice, I had to do something!'

'Regardless, you should have spoken with me before embarking on that journey. Black Annis may have passed over at this early stage in the Shadowing, but she will grow increasingly strong – and increasingly *dangerous* – with each feeding.' The ghost paused. 'Nevertheless,' he said, 'you showed great courage in your actions. And we know you have discovered and used new powers. You showed strength and focus when it mattered most. That is good.'

Callum shrugged. 'It didn't help that girl.'

'No,' Jacob said. 'But you saved Melissa's life.'

'Yeah,' Callum said, but he couldn't help feeling depressed. He had already allowed people to die at the hands of this demon. And she was just the first to cross over.

He *had* to do better, or . . . He didn't know if he even wanted to think about the other option. 'What if I can't actually do what I'm going to need to do?' he murmured.

Jacob walked over to Callum and looked him dead in the eye. 'Would you rather hide? Leave the world to these monsters – and these humans who wish to do their own kind harm?'

Callum held Jacob's gaze for a moment, and then shook his head. He folded his arms and frowned, recalling again how his mother said that attitude makes all the difference.

'No.'

Jacob nodded, and kept his eyes on Callum a moment longer before speaking. 'Good. Good. Now, you say that this group of humans seemed united?'

Callum went over the vision once again. Jacob's figure seemed to be melding into the growing darkness, but Callum could see the look of concern on his face.

'I fear they are a coven,' Jacob said finally. 'And I fear you may be correct, that they were making a sacrifice of Black Annis. The consequences could be severe.'

'Like . . . like what exactly?' Callum wasn't sure if he wanted to know the answer.

'As I said, Black Annis is a dangerous crone – particularly if she is feeding regularly.' Jacob stopped for a moment, and seemed to be considering something. After a moment, he continued. 'There is usually only one reason for sacrificing a Netherworld demon . . . To widen a gap in the Boundary.'

'Widen?' Callum repeated. 'So they might be trying

to bring something bigger over?'

'Something bigger or more powerful. Or perhaps even a greater quantity of demons sooner,' Jacob replied. 'Either way, an increase in demonic activity before you are fully prepared is very bad news.'

Callum let out a wry laugh – he hardly needed telling.

'We need to get to Black Annis before they do, then,' he said determinedly.

Jacob shook his head. 'I fear it will not be so easy, Callum. Black Annis is not like the Fetch. She is more intelligent. Now that she is aware you are seeking her out, she will lie low – so low we may not be able to find her again. You cannot search the whole of Leicester in the hopes of stumbling across her.'

Callum's heart sank.

'OK,' he sighed. 'Well then for now we'll just have to concentrate on getting my powers up to scratch.'

'Certainly. However, I think you have had the best possible practice for today.'

'Come on, Jacob, I need to do this,' Callum pressed, but Jacob held up his hands.

'I think you must go home, have some time to

digest what has happened. We shall return to our tutorials tomorrow.'

Callum was a little irritated, but he had a feeling Jacob was right. There was a tumult of emotions swirling around his mind, and he wasn't sure how much more he'd be able to handle today. 'Fine. I'll see you tomorrow then.'

Callum turned to leave, but he stopped as Jacob called his name.

'One more thing,' the Born Dead said. 'Something you must be alert for, now that we have more evidence of a mortal conspiracy within the Shadowing.'

Callum turned, waiting.

'They may try to enlist you,' Jacob said at last. Callum raised an eyebrow.

'To join the Dark Side?' he said sarcastically.

'It is no joking matter,' Jacob said, his face solemn. 'Callum, you would make a powerful tool for the coven, and indeed for Netherworld forces themselves, if you allied yourself with them willingly. As you are now aware, some mortals do so without hesitation.'

Callum smiled   for the first time that day, it

seemed. 'Jacob, that's one thing I don't think we have to worry about.'

But the Born Dead's black eyes were deadly serious. 'Do not underestimate the power you wield, Callum. Do not underestimate the temptations that the coven may lay in front of you.'

Callum paused for a moment, then nodded silently and made his way out of the graveyard. Jacob's words were still turning over in his mind as he walked back to the cottage.

He pushed his hands deeper into his pockets. All he knew was that he needed to do *something* now. With Black Annis still on the loose, the humans from his vision were a step closer to doing whatever it was they planned to do, and that was his fault. Callum vowed not to make the same mistake again.

Next time, he'd be ready.

Chapter Fourteen

Black Annis feels the weight of this strange, changed world on her shoulders. She has been feeding steadily, and she grows stronger. But things are not as simple as they used to be. The children are more plentiful in this modern mortal world, but they are also more carefully guarded. They sleep behind bars and sheets of glass and locked doors. The very effort of getting to her prey makes her hunger more intense. Yes, things used to be easier.

And the chime child.

Black Annis sighs and looks around at the walls of her lair with her glowing eyes. Already she feels the need to tear flesh from bone once more – as her strength grows, she feels an increasing compulsion to feed. She would never have resorted to snatching a child from the streets in broad daylight otherwise. And now she has been detected by a chime child. Annis shakes her head. She cannot afford such risks any longer. This local guardian is certainly a threat — the boy cannot have faced a great number of adversaries so soon in the dark time, and yet he was fearless and strong. He had even managed to inflict an injury . . . Black Annis reaches up to her cheek, where the wound still gapes. Yes, she cannot underestimate this boy.

Black Annis reaches down to her skirts, unties the fresh pelt and unfurls it slowly. Studying the skin carefully, she holds it up to her mouth and gnaws at the last pieces of flesh. Licking her blue-black lips, Black Annis stretches out the pelt, now stripped clean, and hangs it out to dry next to the others.

It could well be her last meal for a while.

Chapter Fifteen

Callum stood in the cramped kitchen of the cottage
and winced at the ear splitting noise of the food
processor whirring into life. He could kind of relate to
the carrots and onions that were being pulverised into
soup. It was the day after his encounter with Black
Annis in the alleyway, and he'd arrived home from his
training session with Jacob feeling as though he'd
been put through a blender himself.

Every muscle in his body ached, and he'd been
concentrating so hard that he could almost feel his
brain throbbing.

Jacob seemed pleased with his progress, but try as

he might, Callum hadn't been able to recreate the burst of energy he'd produced the previous day. Without perfecting that, he couldn't believe he'd have a chance at stopping Black Annis, or the coven.

Callum switched off the food processor and heard an agitated voice coming from the other room.

'Callum!' Gran shouted, her voice lowering as the machine fell silent. 'Finally! I thought my eardrums were going to burst. I never saw what was wrong with a good boiling and a potato masher,' she said, coming to the kitchen doorway with a smile. Callum didn't return it. The food processor was one of the few modern appliances that his mother had left behind when she died – Callum wasn't about to stop using it.

'It's quicker this way,' he muttered. It had been Gran's turn to cook, but her session teaching Melissa had still been going strong when Callum arrived home, and he was starving. Gran raised an eyebrow at Callum's obvious bad mood, but they were interrupted by Melissa's excited squeal.

'Mrs Scott, I did it! Come and look!'

Gran turned back towards the living room and

Callum grimaced. Melissa was clearly still taking to her magic lessons like a duck to water. He rolled his eyes as another shout came a moment later.

'Callum! Come and see my floating spell!'

'In a minute,' he shouted, but he doubted that Melissa would register his annoyance. Sighing, he put down the knife and wiped his hands on a dishcloth slowly before going into the living room.

'Go on then,' he said.

There was a yellow pencil lying on the table in front of Melissa. Squinting hard, she concentrated on it until the pencil began to wobble a little. She took a breath and refocused, and Callum noticed that her brow was shining with sweat. It was clearly taking some effort, but then finally the pencil began to float into the air as if pulled by an invisible string. It stayed suspended a little distance in front of her face for about ten seconds, before clattering back on to the table.

'How cool is that?' she exclaimed. Even Gran couldn't suppress a smile. But Callum just felt his mood getting even worse.

'Yeah,' he muttered. 'Nice one. I'm going to finish the soup.'

Callum turned back to the kitchen and went over to the chopping board. OK, making a pencil float wasn't as impressive as blasting supernatural energy from your hands, but it was just irritating how quickly Melissa was getting the hang of what was expected of her. He began to dice some more onions. As he angrily sliced into a vegetable the blade slipped, slashing a deep gash across the thumb of his left hand. He stifled a cry, taking in a sharp breath as the pain flashed through him. He was about to call out to his gran for a bandage when he had an idea.

This was exactly what he needed: an opportunity to practise his healing power.

Blood was seeping between his fingers as he pressed at the wound trying to stop the flow. Callum swallowed and moved over to the sink quickly. Concentrating hard, he tried to bring on the prickling sensation in his hands. But try as he might, nothing was happening. The blood now dripped in big, rapid splashes into the old enamel sink, vivid red splattering against its off-white surface. The vase of wilting peonies that Gran had placed on the windowsill to catch the afternoon light began to double in his vision.

He had to do something fast.

Come on . . . heal! Callum thought, taking a deep breath. Closing his eyes, he tried to concentrate on that single thought. Slowly, he felt a slight tingling begin in his fingertips. Was it just the pain in his thumb, or was his power really beginning to work? Callum edged his eyelids open and, to his relief, he saw the strange shimmering energy starting to flow over his left hand from his right. Trying to hold his concentration, he urged more power towards the wound. Before his eyes, the line of blood began to disappear as the skin of his thumb sealed itself once more. Callum waited until the blood had definitely stopped dripping before he took his hand away. Sure enough, his hand was still chapped and rough from the cold, but there was now only a small incision where the deep cut had been. It wasn't totally healed like Melissa's wound had been, but it was a start.

'Not bad,' he whispered to himself, and flicked on the tap to wash away the blood that had stained his fingers.

'Did you cut yourself?'

Gran's voice behind him made Callum jump. 'Goodness, that's a lot of blood. Are you OK? Let me have a look.'

'Uh . . . no, it's fine, it looks worse than it is,' he said, glancing at the splashes on the countertop and chopping board. 'I'll clean that up.'

Callum swiftly proffered his hand for Gran to inspect and then grabbed some plasters from the cupboard. 'Dinner's almost ready,' he said with a smile. For once it felt genuine. He'd actually used a power at will; thought about doing something and made it happen.

'Gosh, a spell in the sun has done these flowers a world of good!' Gran was saying. Callum turned around and, to his surprise, the peonies – which only moments ago had looked bedraggled and limp – were now standing proudly in the vase, their petals vivid as the day they were cut.

'Uh, yeah, looks like it,' Callum replied, frowning a little. Perhaps some of his power had spilled out on to the flowers? That could be why the cut hadn't fully healed. Jacob had said it's all about focus . . . Still, even if he hadn't used his power perfectly, it was a start.

'Well, I'm glad to see your mood has improved,' Gran said. 'Melissa's nearly finished for today.'

Callum waited, expecting Gran to go back into the living room, but she hesitated. 'Callum . . .' she began, then sighed. 'I know things have been a bit difficult between us lately, but I want you to know you can talk to me.'

Callum felt his smile fading – he had a feeling he knew where this was leading. He really didn't want to have a heavy conversation right now.

'Yeah, I know that,' he said quickly. He turned back to pour the soup from the processor into a pot on the stove and began to stir emphatically, hoping it would put Gran off. But it didn't work.

'Have you . . . have you come up against anything yet? I mean, anything strange? Have you discovered anything new yet? I mean in terms of you being . . .'

Callum huffed – he wouldn't even know where to begin. 'You mean in terms of me being a chime child? Look, Gran, I'm not trying to be awkward, but I think it's better if we *don't* talk about that. Don't worry, OK? I'll be fine.'

'Have you been going over the books?'

Callum shrugged. 'Melissa was meant to help me with it again this evening, but I guess you both lost track of time.'

Just then, he saw Melissa emerge behind his grandmother in the small sitting room with an apologetic look on her face. 'Callum, I'm so sorry – I'm meant to be babysitting tonight otherwise I'd stay. Maybe at school tomorrow we can go over some stuff?'

Gran turned around to give Melissa a warning stare, but Melissa held up her hands in protest.

'Well, obviously I won't have the books with me or anything, Mrs Scott! I'll be careful. Nobody will know . . .' She tailed off as she glanced over and Callum gave her a glare of his own. All he needed was another reason for Gran to fret over their every move.

'I'll see you on Saturday, Melissa,' was Gran's only

reply, though her look still bore a warning.

'Hang on,' Callum called as Melissa made her way to the door, then he turned to his grandmother. 'Uh, Gran, I don't suppose you could finish off the soup? The bread's in the oven.' He hadn't had a chance to speak to Melissa alone about what Jacob had told him the previous day. Gran nodded mutely and pursed her lips. Callum pulled on a jacket and followed Melissa outside.

'I'll just be a sec,' he called over his shoulder before shutting the front door. He hunched his shoulders against the cold and turned to Melissa who was standing expectantly on the porch. Her feathered scarf threw abstract shadows on the floor behind her under the light of the bulb above them.

'So what did our Born Dead friend have to say about what happened in Leicester?' she asked. Callum pressed a finger to his lips – he didn't want Gran overhearing anything.

'It's bad,' he said quietly. 'Not only do we have a demon on the loose who is going around eating kids, but Jacob thinks that my vision might mean these humans – a coven, he called them – that they might be planning to sacrifice Black Annis as a way of widening one of the gaps in the Boundary.'

'*Seriously?*'

Callum nodded. 'They might be hoping to bring more dangerous . . . stuff . . . over from the Netherworld sooner than we thought.'

Melissa's eyes widened with shock. 'Oh.'

'There's another problem,' Callum said with a frown. 'He said that my fight with Black Annis may have driven her into hiding. She'll be much harder to find, which means stopping these coven people might be even more difficult.'

Melissa sighed heavily. 'Fabulous,' she said dejectedly. She looked up. 'But you did what you had to, Callum. She could have killed me! And at least it might buy us some time while she's not out there hurting kids.'

Callum nodded, but remained silent.

'I don't suppose you've had any more visions yet?' Melissa said. 'If something as big as widening a gap in the Boundary was about to happen, and with these new premonitions, I would have thought you'd get a warning?'

'Nothing more, not yet anyway.'

'Well, that's good, right?' Melissa said, though her face still looked worried.

'Yeah, I just wish I felt better prepared,' Callum said, pressing his hands into his armpits. 'You seem to be getting on well though.' He couldn't keep the hint of jealousy out of his voice, but once again Melissa seemed oblivious.

'Callum, I bet you're doing better than you think. I mean, I can't believe how much Gran's already taught *me*. She told me I'm a natural, and that's high praise coming from her. And look, tomorrow I'll go over more chime child stuff with you. It'll be cool, we'll catch up. Sorry, I know I've been neglecting it a bit, but it's just so exciting learning some *real magic*, it's, like –'

'Melissa!' Callum interrupted before steam began to come out of her ears. He'd never met anyone better at rambling. 'Uh, it's kind of cold out here, in case you hadn't noticed,' he said with a grin. 'We'll talk at school though.'

'Oh, of course. Sorry! See you tomorrow, Callum.'

She waved and made her way down the steps. Callum shook his head. If only he had as much faith as Melissa did that this would all work out fine. Gratefully, he returned to the warmth of the cottage – and Gran's worried gaze.

'Callum,' she said.

'Yeah?'

'What I meant to say to you earlier was – just be careful, OK?'

Callum was about to retort, but he stopped himself. He knew Gran was just concerned, and he didn't want to totally shut out the person who he knew deep down cared most about him. Especially when he was trying to prepare for an apocalypse.

He took a deep breath and tried for a smile. 'I'll do my best.'

On all fronts, he thought to himself grimly.

Chapter Sixteen

A few days passed, and nothing out of the ordinary happened. No more clues about Black Annis or the coven. Callum thought it was a bit ironic that he was so desperate to hear what would essentially be bad news, but all the waiting and not knowing was really starting to get to him.

School seemed even more mundane than usual, given what he was facing, other than teachers warning the students to be careful given the spate of young people going missing from Leicester. But as Callum was stuffing his maths book into his bag after class, he noticed the two boys near him had their heads bent together while they gathered up pencils and paper.

'Yeah, it was *dead weird*,' one said. 'We were just coming along the Stockport Road, you know by the industrial estate, at the big roundabout? Well, Dad slowed up to wait for the traffic, and these two little girls in long grey dresses ran right across the road in front of us. They didn't look, just *ran* right across the road. Dad slammed on the brakes and honked his horn but they *still* didn't look. It was like they couldn't see or hear us at all. Like they didn't even know there were any cars around them.'

'Travellers, maybe?'

'Traveller kids don't dress like nuns! And the other weird thing was that when I looked up the drive they'd just *vanished*. There isn't really anywhere to hide there. It was like they'd completely disappeared.'

'Ghosts!'

Both boys laughed nervously.

If only they knew, Callum thought. So Melissa really wasn't the only ordinary person who was starting to see apparitions. The Shadowing was starting to affect everybody. Even without the threat of the coven and Black Annis, things were stirring in the Netherworld, and Callum would need to fight them – not just in Marlock and Leicester but everywhere. Probably all over the world. Callum swallowed, trying not to let his thoughts overwhelm him. Pushing his seat back as the second bell went, he quickly made his way to his English class.

He was late anyway, and as he sat down next to Melissa, she mouthed, 'You OK?'

Callum nodded, but was interrupted by Mrs Higgins at the front of the class.

'Nice of you to join us, Mr Scott,' she said, raising an eyebrow. 'Now, if you'd all like to open your textbooks to page fifteen. In fact, Mark, Richard, why don't you two come up here and act it out for us?'

The two boys made their way to the front of the classroom and began to struggle through the Shakespearean text. After a few minutes, Callum saw Melissa reach over and pass him a note.

You look knackered. Like that leathery demon thing from the chime child books yesterday!

She'd written with a smiley face, underneath five lines of notes on *Much Ado About Nothing*. Callum chuckled, but then tried to cover as the teacher looked over, pretending to be amused by the scene his classmates were enacting. He hoped it was meant to be from a comedy.

Callum scribbled an answer below Melissa's message.

Stress! Still no visions. Heard Tom & Ben laughing about seeing ghosts just now too. Feel like something's coming, but don't know what to do about it.

Melissa answered back almost immediately.

It's good they didn't really believe it. Did Jacob have any ideas?

Callum glanced over at what she'd written and shook his head.

Melissa shrugged as she carried on writing.

We still have time though, C. You've got the hang of healing and shield, right?

Callum read quickly and then scribbled back:

Kind of. Just hate all this waiting around.

Callum didn't use written communication much – he had no computer at home and no mobile phone, and no one to send letters to anyway. It surprised him how much writing his worries down helped.

If only there was some way to draw Annis out . . .

Are we too old to act as bait for her?!! Melissa wrote.

Callum raised his eyebrows and shook his head disapprovingly, flipping the sheet over to continue on the back. He'd completely lost focus on anything to do with school, English, or Shakespeare . . .

Don't even joke. You saw what she did to that girl. Seriously, this is not good. Need a breakthrough, and soon.

He slid the page back across to Melissa's desk, and she nodded at him with a more sombre look on her face. She bent over the paper to write.

I know. Well, it's Sat tomorrow. Am due round at yours again for magic lesson, and we can do a good sesh on chime child books too.

Callum read Melissa's note, then glanced over at her and shrugged. It was all they could do really. Melissa beckoned, as if she wanted the page back so she could add something to it, and Callum picked it up to hand it to her.

'CALLUM SCOTT!'

A copy of *Much Ado About Nothing* came slamming down on Callum's desk, pinning down the sheet of paper. Callum jumped and looked up to see his English teacher standing in front of him, seething.

Mrs Higgins wasn't one of Callum's favourite teachers. She was a tall, thin woman, and a real stickler for rules.

'Taking notes on the *play*, are you, Callum?' Mrs Higgins asked with icy sarcasm.

Callum stared up at the teacher mutely, too startled to lie.

'They're *my* notes, Mrs Higgins,' Melissa injected quickly.

Mrs Higgins glanced at her. Melissa might be the class oddball at times, but she was one of the top English students in their year, and rarely gave the teachers any grief.

'Is that so?' Mrs Higgins said suspiciously.

'Yes. Callum asked to see them. We're only reading through the play at the moment, right? It's not a test or anything. I thought it would be OK to show him. I mean, there isn't much there, I guess maybe it's not worth his while going over it yet –'

'I'll take that,' Mrs Higgins demanded, glaring at Callum and ignoring Melissa's reasoning. Callum felt panic rising in his stomach. He and Mrs Higgins both reached for the sheet of paper. Callum would have crunched it into a ball and hurled it out the window, if necessary, to avoid his teacher – or anyone else – reading it. They'd been so careless, what were they thinking?

But, to Callum's surprise, Melissa smoothly pulled the page from his desk a second before either Callum's or the teacher's fingers touched it. With the wrong end of her pencil she made a rapid, sweeping gesture over the page, as though she were pretending to rub something out.

Then with quiet confidence, as Mrs Higgins stretched her hand toward her, Melissa handed the teacher the sheet of paper without protest. Callum clenched his teeth and his fists. He sat and waited, looking down at his desk and feeling his cheeks burning furiously as Mrs Higgins scanned the page.

After a moment, Callum heard the sheet of paper

being flipped over as the teacher glanced at the other side. Then she tossed the piece of paper down on Callum's desk and walked back to the front of the class.

'Go on, Mark. Sorry about the interruption. From: *"Everyone can master grief but he that has it."'*

Callum looked at his desk and gasped. He couldn't believe it. Apart from those five original lines Melissa had written about the opening of the play, the page was entirely blank.

Chapter Seventeen

Flames flicker at the feet of the human magic-users who assemble once more in their meeting place. It has been ten days since they gathered last. The coven members regard one another solemnly, until finally their leader speaks.

'So far, our preparations have gone to plan,' Varick begins, his voice echoing around the cold, empty space. 'Soon our ceremony can take place, and the unknown measures of power that await us all shall finally be revealed. When the Demon Lord treads upon mortal soil, there will be no end to the time of the Shadowing.'

'Soon may he come,' the other coven members chant eagerly. Varick holds up his hands.

'But first, brothers and sisters,' he says, 'there is one final element that we require. The most important of all.'

The others nod, but then the grey-haired woman speaks up.

'Brother Varick, would it not be possible to seize the crone direct from inside her lair? We know the entryway. Surely we could take her by surprise?'

'Maeve, someone of your years of experience should know that things are never as simple as they seem,' the red-headed woman, Aradia, interjects, her beautiful emerald eyes glinting in the candlelight.

Maeve frowns at the younger woman but says nothing. She knows that speaking out against Varick's chosen deputy could mean dismissal from the coven, and she does not wish to risk such a thing when their goal is so close at hand.

'Aradia is right,' Varick says. 'We must not underestimate Black Annis' power and cunning. She crossed over, just as we had hoped, at the start of the

Shadowing, but she has lain low now for quite some time – something has thrown her into a state of caution. Her lair will almost certainly be difficult to penetrate. No, what we need is subtlety. We must lure the hag with . . . *bait.*' Varick turns to Aradia.

'I trust you are up to the task?'

'Of course,' Aradia purrs.

*

The boy in the supermarket is around six years old. His chestnut hair forms thick curls, offsetting large, round blue eyes from which fat tears are spilling. His father is doing his best to ignore the child's loud cries.

'No means *no*, Leonard!' the man says to his son at last, but the boy is relentless, picking up a large, silver-wrapped chocolate bar once more.

'I want it!' he shouts, but his father calmly removes the bar from the boy's hands and replaces it on the shelf.

'What did I *just* say? Stop it, now.' The man turns and begins to browse the shelves further down the aisle, leaving his son to run out of tears. He does not see the tall, beautiful woman with the long red hair watching them from a distance in the store. She makes no pretence of shopping for groceries. She observes the boy carefully, her arms folded.

She has chosen him.

The boy's sobs continue unabated, but his round eyes soon fall on the red-headed woman. She smiles slowly and presses one long, perfectly manicured finger to her lips.

'Shhh,' she says. The boy instantly quietens, though tears still drip down his face. 'That's it,' she says in a low voice. She knows the child can hear her, although she is at least fifteen metres away from him. She pauses for a moment as the boy's father speaks again – but he does not look round.

'*Finally* – thank you! This doesn't mean I'm not going to tell your mum about how badly you've been behaving . . .'

The red-headed woman removes her finger from her lips and holds her hand out in front of her. With a flick of her wrist, something begins to move off the shelf and float towards the boy. Something shiny and silver.

The child gasps with excitement and reaches out to grab the chocolate bar as it moves through the air away from him. He takes a few steps towards the floating chocolate and then stops. He knows it is wrong. He turns to look at his father, and then back at the treat suspended in the air. He opens his mouth to speak, but the moment he does so, the woman frowns and balls her outstretched hand into a fist.

The boy's own hand flies up to his face and clamps over his mouth, stopping his words.

'I said, *shhh*,' the woman hisses.

The child's eyes widen with panic, but he makes no noise. His feet take him slowly, silently, steadily towards the woman – it is as if he is unable to stop himself taking the steps.

It is only when the boy has disappeared from view that his father looks around and sees that his son is gone.

'Leonard?' the man calls. His throat is tight. 'LEONARD?'

It is no use.

Aradia has him now.

Chapter Eighteen

It was a novelty to actually be going to *rugby* practice, rather than trying to practise his chime child abilities with Jacob. Callum walked out of the changing rooms into the crisp air. The sun had barely made an appearance all day. Still, he felt he could use the exercise and the fresh air – it might inspire him, doing something he actually knew he was good at. And it might fend off the growing worry that if they didn't get some clues soon, something terrible could take them all by surprise.

'Come on, Scott,' one of his team-mates called. 'First time you've been to practice in days and you're already running late.'

But Callum saw the familiar figure of Melissa striding towards them as he headed to the pitch.

'I'll be there in a minute,' he said. He jogged over to where Melissa was standing, her cheeks rosy from the wind whipping across the open field.

'What's up?' Callum asked.

'I've been thinking about this whole Black Annis situation,' Melissa said in a low voice, her eyes shining. 'I have an idea.'

Callum raised an eyebrow suspiciously. Something told him that whatever Melissa's idea was, it was going to involve something unorthodox at best, and downright dangerous at worst.

Still, he'd take anything if it meant they'd get things moving.

'Go on then,' he said, folding his arms.

'Not here,' Melissa replied, looking over Callum's shoulder at a couple of the boys who were watching them talk. 'But basically, I think we've been too passive, just waiting for answers. What we need to do is seek them out.' She smiled mysteriously.

Callum frowned.

'Hmm, OK. I'll look forward to hearing this grand scheme later then.'

'Yeah, I'll see you at the cottage,' Melissa said. Then she turned and with a tense wave, hurried back across the field.

As Callum jogged back over to the other boys they laughed and made kissing noises. Callum shook his head and smiled. They were totally off the mark, but Callum decided it was better that they had the wrong end of the stick than knew what he and Melissa were really talking about. He just hoped that Melissa's idea would be the thing to get their search started again. Before it was too late.

*

It is the turning point of the night. The dark, quiet moment when one day becomes the next while mortals sleep. Black Annis crouches alone in her lair. The ancient earth around her, which was once a welcoming home, now seems like a taunting prison. Black Annis is weak with hunger, and very close to breaking her cover and striding out into the world once more to claim another child.

She is almost salivating at the thought. Her talons flex and stretch anxiously. But, suddenly, something draws her out of her reverie. Her gnarled nose twitches. There is a smell wafting down the tunnel and into her lair. It is faint, but Black Annis' sharp senses still pick it up. Could she be deceived, or is that . . .?

She stands up, her skirt of dried skins rustling around her bony legs. She doesn't quite dare to hope, but the smell grows stronger now, closer. Black Annis scrambles up the tunnel towards the entrance to her lair. She sniffs the air fervently, her teeth clattering together involuntarily at the thought of a meal straying so near, at so opportune a moment.

She hesitates only for a second before emerging from the ground and out into the open. The air outside is filled with the smell of the child, but she cannot see it at first. Then Black Annis' eyes alight on a boy. He is a prime specimen, plump, his blue eyes wide. Black Annis' own eyes narrow — what luck would gift her such a prize? She looks left and right, but can see nothing. Suspicion takes hold at the edge of her mind, but Black Annis' desire is powerful to resist. She springs towards the boy, and with one deft movement she pierces his heart. Her teeth sink deep into the child's neck and blood oozes instantly from the wound. His body falls limp; death is immediate.

Euphoria floods through the demon as she clutches the corpse. She sucks at it with fevered hunger. Delicious.

Somewhere in the haze of her desperate feeding, Black Annis realises that she must take the boy down to her lair. The circumstances of the boy straying so close are making her uneasy. However, as she moves to return to the entrance of her lair in the ground, she butts against what feels like an invisible wall. She moves back, and again bumps into some unseen barrier. She is unable to move more than a step in each direction. She lets go of the boy and his body slumps to the ground. Her pale eyes narrow, baffled. What magic is this? Panic rises in the demon's bony chest.

Black Annis whirls around as she hears a voice behind her.

'Do not resist, Black Annis,' a man says calmly. 'You

should conserve your energy.' The hag sees four other humans step out of the shadows to stand beside him. She can feel that it is their united power that maintains the invisible cage.

'Release me,' Black Annis hisses. She pushes furiously against the unseen barrier, clawing at it with her sharp talons. But the snare is strong — too strong for her to break through in her weakened state. The man shakes his head and taps his chin as he regards her. Black Annis sees a large ring on the man's finger; a magical totem. She glares at him as he speaks again.

'Black Annis, we seek your assistance. In return for your help, we can supply you with all the flesh you could desire. And you will not have to lift one beautifully manicured finger.' The man pauses, and smiles. 'In fact, you won't be able to.'

Though Black Annis does not understand all of his words, she knows the man is pleased with himself. The woman next to him, the one with hair the colour of blood, laughs alongside him.

'Black Annis obeys no one,' the crone snarls.

'Oh, but you will. You see that we have brought you

a sacrifice? And we can bring you many more. Fret not, we shall take care of everything. This will all be for the greater good.'

The man clenches his fist, and the invisible barrier surrounding Black Annis tightens – she feels it pressing in on her. She writhes and struggles, but to no avail. Anger and frustration well up inside her, but Black Annis eventually stops resisting. She must chose her moment . . .

'Good. That's settled then,' the man says, his words coming through gritted teeth. He turns to the other members of his coven. 'Take her inside,' he commands. Black Annis feels her feet leave the ground as the group raises their hands, and their human magic begins to drag her back down inside her own tunnel to her own lair. The stench of their adult bodies sullies the place Black Annis once called home.

The woman with the hair of blood turns to her leader.

'I'll get to work then, shall I?' she says with a slow smile. The man nods, and the woman turns and heads back up through the tunnel scratched out by Black Annis' bare hands.

'Now,' the man says, turning back towards the crone.

'You must finish your meal.'

They dump the stiffening body of the boy they had lured Black Annis with at her feet. The boy's blood still drips down Black Annis' chin. She is too hungry to protest. Swiftly, silently, she goes about ripping into his cooling flesh until nothing remains but his clean, white bones and a beautiful pure pelt.

Chapter Nineteen

Callum jogged back to the cottage after rugby practice and let himself in, his bare legs blue and red from perishing cold. The extreme weather had even begun to make the national news. There was a picture in the morning paper of people standing on the ice in the middle of the Manchester Ship Canal – as well as reports of another child going missing, this time in broad daylight from a supermarket. Maybe Black Annis had re-emerged, but Callum wasn't sure. Snatching a girl on the street and dragging her into an alleyway was one thing, but going into a *supermarket* and stealing a child seemed an unlikely choice for a Netherworld demon. Still, if Black Annis had started her killing spree again, he needed to stop her, and fast. As he walked into the cottage, Gran and Melissa were sitting at the table in front of the wood fire, looking intense.

'Still playing with the radio?' Callum enquired, putting down his rucksack.

'No, no, we've moved on from that,' Gran said distractedly, rearranging things on the table in front of them.

'I'll show you!' Melissa said eagerly. 'Watch this, Callum!'

In front of them on the table was a pile of short, broken twigs. Melissa shook back the curly hair from around her face and concentrated. Her expression was focused, but also filled with radiant excitement. She reached towards the twigs slowly, but without hesitation, like someone reaching out to stroke an unfamiliar cat.

She didn't do anything obvious. She didn't mutter an incantation or wave her hands about to weave a spell. But she grasped the handful of twigs and rolled them between her palms for a moment as if testing them out.

'These twigs are rowan – protection against evil magic, remember?' she murmured. 'Now, watch this.'

She moved her fingers deftly, weaving the twigs into a little mat. This was the kind of thing Callum would have expected his artistic grandmother to be able to do, but she'd obviously taught Melissa well.

She began to stretch the small wooden trellis by pulling at the ends of the twigs. It was as though they were made of Plasticine. Callum caught his breath. It was amazing. In less than a minute, Melissa was holding what was more or less a shield the size of a tea tray.

'See? Simple protection against evil. I can't make a barrier out of energy, like you can – I've got to use something physical to create wards. Just the way your gran does with the charmed herbs and plants in your garden, you know? But I've got to learn how to weave a deeper spell of protection into the shield. At the moment it's really just an overgrown rowan screen, pretty tame really. Although the magic I used to make it was pretty impressive, right?'

Callum nodded. 'Yeah, pretty impressive!' he said with a smile. 'Anyway, we should probably do a little more work on the chime child books before you have to get home. We could go up to my room, get out of Gran's hair . . . if that's OK with you Gran?' he asked, though he didn't wait for an answer. Picking up a couple of the books from the table, Callum gestured to Melissa and they both headed up the narrow stairs to his room. He was dying to know what Melissa's idea was. He put the books down on his bed and he and Melissa sat cross-legged on the floor.

'OK then, let me have it, Miss Mysterious,' Callum said. 'What's your big idea?'

Melissa took a deep breath and looked around her conspiratorially. 'Well,' she began in a low voice, 'obviously you can see that I'm really starting to get the hang of this whole magic thing, right?'

Callum nodded, but said nothing. He wanted to see where she was heading with this.

'I've been thinking – if we can combine my magic with your chime child powers, we could do something special. I think I can try to *make* you have a vision – one that might help us track down Black Annis, or get to the bottom of this coven.'

'What?' Callum said, frowning in confusion. 'Are you serious?'

Melissa sighed impatiently. 'Yes, of course. Look, if we can deliberately trigger a vision in you somehow, then it could give us a head start, or a vital clue sooner, instead of waiting for something bad to kick one off.'

Callum was silent for a moment. Part of him wanted to congratulate Melissa on coming up with such a daring idea, but at the same time alarm bells were ringing.

'I don't know, Melissa. I mean, you've only been learning magic for a little while. I know what you've been doing is impressive, but triggering a vision sounds like something else altogether. I'm not sure.'

'Come *on*, Callum!' Melissa exclaimed, but then lowered her voice again – she was clearly wary of Gran finding out her scheme. Maybe she'd already suggested it to his grandmother and she'd vetoed it.

Somehow the idea of *that* actually made Callum want to try it. He took a deep breath. 'OK. I guess it's not a bad idea, but how exactly do you plan to try and trigger a vision?' he said.

Melissa didn't answer. Instead, she reached for her bag and pulled out two batteries – big ones, like the kind Callum used to put in an old remote control car he had as a kid.

'Uh, that's your answer? You're planning to charge me up?' Callum said with an uneasy grin.

'Something like that,' Melissa replied. 'Hold out your hands.' She placed one of the batteries in each of Callum's palms and then hovered her own hands over them. 'I told you, sometimes it helps to use physical stuff to make the magic happen, right?'

'Yeah.'

'Well I'm going to use the batteries to send a jolt of energy into you, and hopefully that will trigger your chime child powers.'

'OK, hang on a second.' Callum wasn't sure he liked the sound of that idea but, before he could get any further, Melissa had closed her eyes and a look of keen concentration fell over her features.

At first, Callum felt nothing. Then, gradually, the batteries in his hands began to fizzle and heat up. He felt the prickle of an electric shock begin to pierce his hands and he jerked them away suddenly. The batteries fell on to the carpet between them.

'What the –?' he began.

'Callum!' Melissa exclaimed at the same time. 'What did you do that for? It was working!'

'I don't know if it was working but it was definitely hurting my hands,' Callum said, rubbing his palms.

'Don't be such a baby,' Melissa taunted, with a glint in her eye. Callum still fell for it.

'Fine. Again, then,' he said, rolling his eyes and stretching out his hands. This time, he didn't pull away. As the electricity seemed to build in the batteries, he closed his eyes and tried to let the feeling pass through him. He was just beginning to feel his palms tingle when he heard a loud gasp.

Callum opened his eyes to see his gran standing in the doorway to his bedroom. She had a steaming mug of hot chocolate in each hand, and the warm liquid was slopping everywhere as they shook.

'Melissa . . . Callum . . . What on *earth* do you two think you're doing?'

Chapter Twenty

The three of them stared at one another in silence for what felt to Callum like hours. The defiance that had prompted him to agree to Melissa's scheme drained out of him under his grandmother's furious gaze.

At last, Gran spoke again.

'I should have known,' she said through gritted teeth. 'I absolutely should have known. What was I *thinking*, teaching the Craft to a girl who would come up with ludicrous ideas like this?' Gran shook her head emphatically as she spoke. Callum didn't think he'd ever seen her so angry. Gran turned to go back down the stairs, but Melissa jumped up to stop her.

'Mrs Scott, *please*! I'm sorry, but I wouldn't have even tried it if it wasn't really important.'

Gran glared at Melissa so hard that Callum almost thought she was going to throw the hot chocolate over the girl's head.

'Melissa, I don't think –' he began, trying to calm things down, but Gran interrupted.

'I could sense it!' she said angrily. 'The minute I set foot on the stairs, I could sense magic being used, but I thought, "No, Ethel, you must be imagining things". I couldn't bring myself to believe that you would *actually* go behind my back like that, when I've expressly told you not to try any of this without my supervision. After all your promises! You betrayed my trust, Melissa. I knew this was a mistake.'

Melissa stood dumbstruck as Gran thundered back down the stairs. Callum heard her clatter the mugs into the sink in the kitchen. Melissa started down the stairs too, but Callum quickly stood up.

'Don't,' he said. 'Just leave her for a minute. I'll go down and try to talk to her.'

Melissa nodded mutely. She headed back into

169

Callum's room and slumped down on to his bed with a sigh. 'Good luck,' she muttered.

Callum took a deep breath and then slowly made his way downstairs to confront his grandmother. She was still standing in the kitchen, her hands gripping the edge of the sink. She stared out of the window, and Callum could see that the rise and fall of her shoulders was gradually beginning to slow as her angry breaths returned to normal.

'Gran?'

She didn't turn around, but Callum took her silence as a signal that he could keep talking. 'Gran, we weren't trying to deceive you. It's just . . . things are getting kind of serious, and it was a last resort. We needed to do something, before the situation we're facing gets out of control.'

Finally, his grandmother turned around to him and folded her arms. Callum could see that she was considering her words carefully before she spoke.

'Callum, I know that you want to do this on your own, this fight, dealing with the Shadowing. I know that's my fault. That my actions – even though they were intended to be in your best interests – mean you're not as prepared as you might have been. But you have to believe that you *can* talk to me about this. About *anything*. We're family, Callum.'

Callum had been looking down at his trainers as his Gran spoke but, at that, he raised his eyes to meet hers. 'I know, Gran,' he said. 'Of course I do. But if I'd come to you and said, "Hey, Gran, Melissa and I are hoping to trigger one of my chime child visions using magic," would you have said it was a great idea and jumped at the chance to help us?' He could feel a smile playing on his lips, and he could see his gran biting one back as well.

'Fine, I may not have been entirely receptive at first,' Gran conceded. 'But I really am here to help you, Callum. If only you'd let me. Why do you think I agreed to train Melissa, and let her read the chime child books? You wouldn't let me help you directly, so that was the only thing I could do. But magic is *not* something you can mess around with.' She tailed off as she heard Melissa slowly making her way down the stairs. She came into the kitchen, her face solemn.

'I really am sorry, Mrs Scott, and I appreciate everything you've been showing me,' Melissa said quietly, beginning to gather her things. 'I'll understand if you want to stop our lessons now.'

'Wait,' Gran said, finally unfolding her arms. Melissa stopped and turned around.

'You were trying to get Callum to have a *vision* using your magic?' Gran said.

Melissa nodded silently, and then glanced over at Callum.

'And you think this will be important in getting somewhere with the situation you are facing?' Gran continued.

'Yes.' Callum answered for both of them.

Gran turned and looked her grandson in the eye.

'OK,' she said. 'Then I'll help you.'

Her words hung in the air for a moment, and Callum heard Melissa desperately trying to suppress a squeal of excitement. He remained quiet though – he knew there would be a catch.

'On one condition,' Gran said. 'You have to tell me exactly what's going on.'

Callum sighed. He wasn't even sure if triggering a vision would give them anything useful. And was it worth the risk of getting Gran involved, or having her interfere in whatever they decided to do to try and stop Black Annis and the Coven? He looked at his Gran, whose eyebrows were raised expectantly, and then over at Melissa. They were both waiting for an answer.

'OK, OK,' he said finally. 'But, Gran, if we tell you what it is, you have to promise not to try and interfere, or keep *me* from getting involved?'

Gran considered it for a long moment.

'Fine,' she said at last.

Melissa's face burst into a grin, but Callum knew that he would have to be economical with the truth – maybe even bend it a little. As they all sat down at the table in the living room, Callum quickly explained that from some recent visions, he and Melissa had established that a demon witch, Black Annis, had crossed over from the Netherworld at the start of the Shadowing, and that there might be a plot by a human coven to involve the crone in a ritual sacrifice.

He studiously left out any mention of Jacob or Doom, remembering the Born Dead's warnings. Callum was certain, in any case, that now was definitely *not* the time to reveal that he'd been having chime child lessons from a ghost.

'What exactly do you think these magicians plan to achieve by sacrificing Black Annis? Did your vision give any indication about that?' Gran asked, her brows knitted together with concern.

Callum and Melissa exchanged looks.

'We, uh . . . we think that they're planning to widen one of the gaps in the Boundary,' Callum said grudgingly. He wasn't sure if revealing the gravity of the situation would help or hinder their case in getting Gran to assist them.

'Widen it?' Gran said incredulously.

'Yes,' Callum said grimly. 'We think they might be planning to bring more – or bigger – demons across, and sooner than we were expecting. So we've got even less time to prepare than we thought.'

'Oh my goodness,' Gran breathed.

'Exactly,' Callum said wryly. 'Melissa just thought

that, as things have gone quiet, if she could help me have one of my premonitions it might give us some clues about how to stop it.'

Callum waited, letting the idea sink in. He braced himself for Gran to freak out and tell him they were packing up and moving to Timbuktu, but she just sat for a moment, thinking.

'Right,' Gran said at last. 'Give me your hands.'

'What?' Melissa replied, but Gran reached out and clasped her own hands around one of Melissa's and one of Callum's. She indicated that they should link hands too.

'Doing something of this nature with magic will require a Three in any case,' Gran said. 'You'd never have been able to do it properly on your own, Melissa. Such a thing requires control and focus.'

With nothing more than that, Gran closed her eyes and began to chant. Both Callum and Melissa stared at her dumbfounded for a moment before Callum saw Melissa follow suit and close her eyes as well. Soon Melissa began to repeat the strange phrase that his grandmother was saying over and over again.

They gripped Callum's hands tightly and after a moment, to his shock, Callum's palms began to tingle uncontrollably.

He stared at Melissa and Gran as their lips moved faster and faster, their voices becoming almost indistinguishable, their heads bowed in complete concentration.

And then everything went black . . .

Chapter Twenty-One

Callum suddenly felt still, almost peaceful.

He could see nothing but blackness, but as he took a deep breath in and out, he realised that the darkness was not *surrounding* him. He was inside a vision – and his eyes were closed. Was he asleep? Yes, for some reason, he felt small and safe, in bed asleep. He felt warm and comfortable, and nothing was wrong at all.

Then Callum heard it.

A voice. A whisper, low in his ear. There was no breath against his cheek, no indication that there was someone in the bedroom with him. And yet he could hear words, so close. They seemed to float into the room through the air, straight towards him, like . . . magic.

'When, lo, as they reached the mountain's side,

A wondrous portal opened wide . . .'

At the sound of the words, Callum's eyes sprang open, almost against his will. He could see a child's bedroom around him, but he hardly registered his surroundings. It was as though he was in a trance. The words echoed around his mind, again and again.

Callum could feel soft, plush carpet beneath his bare feet as he swung over the edge of the bed. He began to walk, zombie-like, towards the bedroom door, and then he felt himself moving through the darkened corridor of the house and straight to the front door, like a puppet controlled by some unseen force.

Callum realised he had to stand on tiptoes to reach the front door latch. But with eerie precision, he opened the locks and strode out into the street. Yellow light pooled in circles on the cold concrete beneath his bare feet, but Callum knew this wouldn't stop him. He was being called, and he was coming . . .

*

Callum came to, shaking his head slightly but otherwise feeling less like he'd had an anvil dropped on his head than he usually did after a vision. Gran and Melissa, on the other hand, were looking far more the worse for wear. They both dropped his hands and sat back, panting. Melissa looked very pale, and her eyes remained unfocused for several moments.

'Did it work?' Gran said between breaths.

'Yeah, sort of,' Callum replied, 'but are you guys OK?'

He looked at Melissa anxiously, who was still breathing heavily, but she nodded and gave him a shaky smile. Gran's expression was grim as she looked over at Melissa's trembling frame.

'We won't be doing that again in a hurry,' she muttered.

'Yeah, that was pretty hectic,' Melissa agreed, colour only just returning to her face. 'But what did you see? Anything useful?'

Callum was almost sorry to tell them after all the

effort they'd clearly gone to, but he really didn't know what to make of the vision he'd had. It certainly didn't seem to give them any solid clues as to how to get to Black Annis or stop the coven.

'Well, it was weird – it definitely wasn't as intense as my normal visions, but there was something pretty strange happening. I felt like I was young, really young . . .'

'Perhaps we triggered some sort of memory instead?' Gran asked.

'No,' Callum said, 'it was definitely a vision. It was as if I was seeing it from someone else's perspective – a kid, and he was under some kind of trance. He was asleep in bed, then there was this weird whisper, and suddenly he got up and walked out of his house into the street, totally . . . zombified.'

Melissa frowned. 'Definitely weird.'

'Can you remember what was whispered?' Gran said.

Callum racked his brain, trying to remember it exactly. 'Yeah, it was, *"When, lo, as they reached the mountain's side; a wondrous portal opened wide . . ."*

That's all I can remember. I don't know what it means though.'

'It doesn't sound good, whatever it is,' Melissa said. 'Maybe the chime child books have some reference to it?'

Callum looked over at Gran. Her brow was furrowed.

'What is it, Gran?'

'I don't know, there's something so familiar about those words, but I just can't quite place them,' she said.

Melissa got up and began rifling through the chime child books, passing volumes to Callum and Gran to look through too. But it was no use – they couldn't find the phrase anywhere.

'We can keep looking tomorrow,' Melissa said. 'It sounds like it must have something to do with Annis or the coven – I mean, "a portal opened wide?"'

Callum nodded. He felt even more baffled and uneasy than he had before. What was happening to the boy in his vision? Where was he, and where was he *going*? More and more questions were piling up in Callum's mind, and he had no idea how to deal with it all. He snapped one of the chime child books shut with a grunt.

'It's getting late,' Gran said, looking over at Callum. 'I think you ought to be getting home, Melissa. Perhaps you should ring your parents to come and collect you?'

'I'll be fine,' Melissa began, but Gran's stern look told her that she wouldn't be allowed to walk home alone tonight, not after everything the older woman had heard that evening. As Melissa pulled out her mobile phone to call home, Callum sighed and turned to his grandmother.

'Thanks for all this, Gran,' he said in a low voice. 'I know it's been a bit of a strain, but we really did need all the help we could get. I just hope we can find out what's going on before it's too late.'

'I do too, Callum,' Gran replied. 'I do too.'

Chapter Twenty-Two

Daylight glints off the flame-red hair of the woman approaching the school gates. She breathes in the fresh air, relishing the relative ease of the task ahead of her. She hears the children's laughing, squealing voices as they play in the concrete grounds, oblivious. And so they shall remain, she thinks.

The adults posted around the gates – the teachers charged with protecting these youngsters – remain unseeing, a result of Aradia's magic. They know nothing of the fate that will befall the children they are supposed to be watching over. As she strides up to the iron railings of the playground, Aradia reads the sign attached to them – ST ANTHONY'S SCHOOL. A smile creeps on to her beautiful face. St Anthony, the patron saint of lost things. *How apt*, she thinks to herself.

She whispers an ancient sequence of words, a spell that will lure a child over to her. A girl of ten or so, with short, slick black hair and honey-brown skin freezes in the middle of the playground. Aradia reaches forwards and crooks her finger. Wordlessly, robotically, the girl turns around and begins to walk towards her. The girl's deep brown eyes are glazed, her expression slack. Aradia leans down to the level of the girl's ear and whispers the special rhyme that she has made into an incantation. It seems so appropriate that *these* are the words that will complete her mission.

She draws herself back up to her full height, and gestures once more. The girl turns, but instead of returning to the gaggle of friends she'd been sharing mobile phone games with, she walks swiftly over to two girls sitting on a step, where one is braiding the other's hair. Aradia folds her arms and watches.

The black-haired girl leans close to each of the

others and whispers straight into their ears. Aradia watches her lips move, and nods slowly.

'Good,' she mutters to herself. She keeps watching as the two girls stop their hair-braiding suddenly. They each move off swiftly and whisper to another two children.

And so it spreads.

Aradia turns on her heel and strides away from the playground.

Chapter Twenty-Three

The dusk air was crisp, and the sky a glowing red as Callum made his way to Gran's cottage. He had barely said two words at school the entire day – all he could think about was the mystery of the vision that Melissa and Gran had helped him generate the previous evening. Even Melissa had seemed subdued in their classes together, with dark circles under her eyes that suggested she'd had just as little sleep as Callum had.

It was almost a relief that Gran had insisted he come home straight from school for once. Part of Callum was annoyed that he wouldn't get the chance to quiz Jacob on the vision, but he was also relieved to have a night off from practising his powers. He was exhausted, and he needed an opportunity to switch his mind off for a while.

But Callum was still feeling distracted as he made his way up the lane . . . until something moving in the corner of his eye brought his mind sharply into focus. Something intangible and misty grey was floating back and forth on one side of the road. Callum turned slowly, warily, and the movement stopped.

Another ghost. Again, this one was unfamiliar, but even though it wasn't as physically threatening the disfigured phantom that had tried to attack Callum and Melissa not so long ago, it was still unsettling. The ethereal, tall wraith was a woman. Her feet didn't seem to touch the ground, but her long, colourless skirts floated round her ankles, and her pale neck was held at a an unnatural angle. Callum swallowed as he saw the dark rope hanging limply around it. She'd been hanged.

He turned to continue down the path, hoping this disturbing spectre would leave him alone, but as he took another step the woman began to float alongside him again. The orange-red light of the setting sun illuminated her with a fiery glow.

'Go away,' Callum said under his breath but, at that, the spirit's black eyes widened.

'Please, please, I'm sorry,' she said, her voice like the wind moving through dried autumn leaves. Callum shivered and quickened his pace doing his best to ignore her. The ghost continued floating alongside him.

'Please!' she said again. 'Please, I did not mean to . . . I did not, it was an accident, I beg of you please, please, help me, I'm stuck here. Help me get away from here, please.'

It was only then that Callum realised she was holding something. He grimaced as she floated in front of him and held the bundle out before her. It was a baby, or the apparition of one – but it did not move. Its eyes were closed and its mouth hung open, slack and motionless.

'STOP!' Callum shouted and rushed forwards. All he wanted was to get away from this nightmarish image. He just wanted to be able to *do* something about it all.

Callum winced as he felt himself pass through an icy

pocket of air. When he turned his head to see what had happened, he realised that he'd run straight through the ghostly woman, who swirled like smoke and then reformed. She stopped following Callum, a crestfallen look on her face. She watched miserably as he hurried away, her head still at its woeful angle, the ghost-baby now cradled limply in her arms.

Callum didn't look back again until he was at the door to the cottage. At least he knew the ghost wouldn't be able to follow him into the house, with all the protective spells Gran kept the cottage cloaked in. Reluctantly, he glanced over his shoulder. The spirit was still looking sadly at him as she drifted backwards down the lane. Callum shivered. Things were getting darker and darker, like a gathering storm, with every day that passed.

But in some strange way the woman's sad, lonely face made Callum think again of his own mother. He missed her more and more each day; his sense of loss felt almost as vivid as it had three years ago. If only he could catch a glimpse of *her* ghost. He needed *something*, some sign that things were going to work out OK.

Maybe Gran's right, Callum thought. *Maybe this was all a mistake and I'm in way over my head?*

He glanced over his shoulder one last time before he stepped inside the cottage. The woman was still drifting slowly back up the path. She left a trail of soft grey mist in her wake. Callum exhaled a lungful of air and quickly opened the door to let himself inside.

He strode straight into the kitchen and poured a glass of water. He'd gulped half of it down before he realised that Gran was sitting in the living room, staring intently at a book on her lap.

'Hey,' he said in surprise. She looked up, and Callum immediately knew something was wrong.

'Callum, I'm glad you're back,' she said, her voice solemn. 'I have a feeling this is something you're going to want to see.'

So much for an evening off, Callum thought as he walked over to see what his grandmother was holding out to him. The book was small and leather-bound, with a worn red cover.

'I remembered where I'd heard the phrase from your vision,' Gran said. 'This is a book of poetry that my own grandmother gave me when I was a young girl. They're poems by Robert Browning.'

Callum read the page that Gran was holding open, and frowned. There, in black and white, were the lines he had heard being whispered mysteriously in his vision:

When, lo, as they reached the mountain's side,
A wondrous portal opened wide,
As if a cavern was suddenly hollowed;
And the Piper advanced and the children followed,
And when all were in to the very last,
The door in the mountain-side shut fast.

Callum looked up in surprise. 'It's about the Pied Piper?' he said.

Gran nodded.

'This really doesn't sound good,' Callum said. 'Luring children away? The kid in my vision was in a trance, being taken off somewhere. That's exactly the sort of thing Black Annis would do.'

Gran took the book back from Callum and stared at

the words again, her lips moving silently as she repeated them to herself.

'Well, we know that even though it's a poem from our world, there must be some link with the Netherworld or the phrase wouldn't have cropped up in your vision.'

'Yeah,' Callum agreed. 'But what could it be?'

'I have a feeling . . . Sometimes, magic can be woven into seemingly innocuous words,' Gran began cautiously. 'I have a feeling that may be what has happened. Someone has worked an enchantment into the words of this poem, something that, if they use them in the right context, will make them into a potentially very powerful spell.'

Callum looked at his Gran, who was pacing back and forth in the small living room, her arms folded, her brow furrowed with shock and concern.

'That could be it,' he said, his mind racing. 'Black Annis could be using a spell to . . . Oh, *no*. Gran, I'd better go and –'

'Callum, please.'

Gran's stern voice stopped Callum in his tracks.

'Wait. Even if it is a spell, what exactly do you think you'll be able to do? *Where* are you going to go? Please, just give me some time to think about it a bit more. You shouldn't do anything rash tonight.'

Callum clenched his teeth. He knew she was right. There was no point trying to do anything right now. Grudgingly, he trudged upstairs and put down his school bag. He could hear Gran starting to make supper downstairs – her answer to most problems was some hearty comfort food. But Callum didn't think there was any food in the world that would comfort him right now. He was itching to get out there, to *do* something. Perhaps this scheme to lure children away had already begun, and here he was waiting for his *supper*?

Callum managed to make it through dinner without leaping up and out of the door. But as soon as Gran began to clear their plates away, he decided there was at least one thing she couldn't object to.

'I'm going to give Melissa a ring,' he said, already stepping over to the old-fashioned telephone and placing one hand on the receiver. 'She's been just as worried about this as I have. I think I should let her know we've found something.'

Callum had already started to dial as Gran nodded and took the rest of the crockery through to the kitchen. He was grateful to hear Melissa's voice at the other end of the line. He hastily explained what Gran had found, and her theory about the words being used as an incantation.

'Really? Blimey,' Melissa breathed. 'But hold on a minute – does it make sense that Black Annis would use such a complicated spell to lure children? It doesn't sound like her style. She's more of a snatch-and-grab type, isn't she?'

'Well, there'd been that kid who was taken from the supermarket, but I've been thinking – there's no way Annis would have been able to just wander in there in broad daylight,' Callum said, his shoulders sagging. 'I know what you mean, a spell like this *is* too subtle for her.'

Then, all of a sudden, something occurred to him. He cupped the mouthpiece and glanced back to the kitchen where his gran was now splashing and clattering as she washed up the dishes.

'Wait a second,' Callum whispered down the phone. 'Jacob said that Black Annis grows stronger the more she feeds, right?'

'Yeah . . .'

'And we know the coven have some purpose for her, from my vision?'

'Mmm . . .'

'Well, what if it's the *coven*? What if *they're* the ones luring children? What if they want to feed her up, make her as strong as possible before they sacrifice her?'

Callum heard Melissa gasp. 'You're right, that would make sense – the more sophisticated magic? How many children are they planning to take? How many are they going to *kill*? Callum what are we going to do?'

'The only thing I can think of right now is to go and speak to Jacob,' Callum said, his heart rate quickening as he heard his grandmother finishing up in the kitchen. 'I'm going to have to sneak out though. Gran's getting really nervy,' he whispered, and then straightened up as his grandmother came back into the room, eyeing him suspiciously.

'Uh, look Melissa, I've got to go,' he said, his voice back to its normal volume.

'OK, but Callum, wait,' she said. 'If you're going to see Jacob, I'm coming with you. Half-past midnight. I'll see you there.'

The dial tone sounded before Callum could protest.

Chapter Twenty-Four

Later that night, Callum hurried through the gate to the churchyard, trying to ignore the gathering, agitated ghosts that watched him as he walked. He skirted round the iron railings of the Victorian graves and the tilting stone skulls of the older ones, finding a place to wait on a ledge where a chapel wall had collapsed. His breath pluming in the cold, he searched the darkness for any sign of Jacob, Doom or Melissa, but there were only the lingering ghosts and the distant hoot of an owl for company.

Then a voice behind him made Callum jump.

'It is rather late for a lesson, is it not?' Jacob stood

with his hands behind his back, his face expectant.

Callum hastily explained how Gran and Melissa had triggered his vision, and what Gran had suggested about the enchanted words. When Callum had finished speaking, Jacob didn't respond immediately. He folded his arms, frowning.

'I agree. It is entirely possible that the words you heard have been spun into some kind of spell,' Jacob said. 'And that it is most likely the work of the coven.'

'How long do you think we have?' Callum asked. 'I mean, if they're luring children . . . How often do you think Black Annis would have to be fed to get to her strongest?' The very thought made him feel sick.

Jacob stood for a moment with one hand twisting the fur at the back of Doom's neck. It was hard to tell from the expression on his pale, faintly gleaming face what he might be thinking. Then he began to pace up and down, shaking his head. Doom stood up and followed.

'I do not know how many –' he began, but then both he and Doom came to a halt as they heard something stirring outside the church gates.

'It's only me,' came a familiar voice, and Callum saw Melissa picking her way towards them. 'So, have we got a plan yet?'

Callum gave her a withering look. 'We don't even really know what's happening, Melissa – or if it's already *happened*.'

'I don't think anything has happened yet though,' Melissa said. 'Surely lots more kids going missing around Leicester would have made the news, just like the others did before?'

Callum frowned. She had a point. 'OK, but if the coven haven't been taking enough kids for the media to notice, then what are we meant to do? Just sit back and wait till more kids start disappearing?'

Melissa shook her head and looked to Jacob anxiously.

'I fear there may be a reason why there have not been reports of many more missing children as yet,' Jacob said slowly. 'If there have not been occasional, *individual* disappearances, then –'

'Then they might be planning to take a whole group of kids all at *once*?' Callum finished. He, Melissa and

Jacob all looked at one another anxiously for a moment as the notion sunk in, then Callum finally spoke again.

'We have to do something, we have to stop them,' he said, folding his arms.

'Like what?' Melissa said. 'We have no idea where they are. How do you expect to stop them?'

'We go to the source. We need to find Black Annis' lair.'

'Callum,' Jacob said. 'I know that you have come on a good deal, but you must realise that this situation could be beyond your control.'

'What choice do I have? It's my job to police the Boundary, isn't it? To keep the world safe? To stop children being skinned and eaten alive, and to stop some crazy group of magicians bringing goodness knows what over from the Netherworld for some premature hell-party.'

Callum raised his eyebrows, inviting a response. Jacob held his gaze for a moment and then sighed, wiping away a trickle of blood that seeped from his hairline like sweat. He beckoned to Doom, and the enormous spectral dog came to lie at Jacob's feet. 'But caution is certainly not folly in this instance. You cannot underestimate how dangerous this could be. And what little power I have myself grows weaker the farther I travel from this village, where I was born and where I lie buried. We must be careful. We are heading into the unknown.'

'We?' Callum said hopefully. Jacob remained silent, his expression serious.

'I do not think this is a good idea,' the ghost said again.

'Why? It's the only place that we have even a remote chance of finding that hag, and it's the most likely place that the coven would go to find her too, if they haven't got her already. We might be able to head them off, or, I don't know . . .'

'I wish there some other way,' Jacob said quietly.

'But there isn't,' Callum said, cutting him short.

Jacob looked up at this. His black, depthless eyes met Callum's straight on. 'At the day's end, chime child, it is only you who can decide which battles you face. Are you sure you want to do this?'

201

Callum tossed his untidy hair back out of his eyes, so that he could return Jacob's challenging gaze head on. He took a deep breath.

'Yes.'

He may not have complete control of his powers, but he could not stand by while children were taken from their beds as snacks for a Netherworld demon.

'Good,' Jacob said. 'If your power is as strong as your resolve, then perhaps you *are* ready.'

Next to them, Melissa cleared her throat. 'This is all very touching, but if we're going to find Black Annis then we should get going.'

'Going *where* though?' Callum said. 'We don't know where her lair is.'

'Well, I read something,' Melissa said, her eyes narrowing. 'It didn't make a lot of sense at the time, but I had a chance to look into it last night after we spoke. There was a fable in one of the chime child books that said there was a tunnel underneath Leicester Castle. One that lead to the den of a "beastly anthropophage".'

'Anthro-what?' Callum said, shaking his head in confusion.

'Turns out it means "flesh-eater". It makes sense, doesn't it? I think it's our best chance.'

'OK,' Callum said, nodding quickly. 'Then we have to try and get there before the coven does.'

'But how exactly do you plan to get to Leicester in the middle of the night?' Melissa asked.

Callum's face fell – but Jacob interjected.

'I think I may be able to assist with that . . .'

Chapter Twenty-Five

The streetlights that line the quiet suburban street begin to wink out, one by one, but the people asleep in their houses remain oblivious. In the middle of the road, three men and two women stand in a line. The shadows they cast are faint in the moonlight, which is now the only source of illumination. Their collective magic has seen to that.

'Are they ready?' the man with the glowing ring asks.

'They are, Varick,' Aradia replies. She brushes her long red hair back from her shoulders, closes her eyes and raises her slender hands out in front of her. She takes a breath and begins to whisper.

'When lo, as they reached the mountain's side . . .'

The four others watch her as she works. The grey-haired woman folds her arms and eyes the younger woman; she is sceptical about the power of Aradia's magic.

But then there is movement.

Almost simultaneously, the doors of the houses on each side of the street begin to open. The red-headed woman keeps whispering, repeating her incantation over and over again. Soon, a dozen children are stepping out on to the street, their feet bare, their eyes glassy and unseeing. The children move slowly towards the five adults gathered in the middle of the street.

'*Excellent* work, Aradia,' Varick says as the children gather in a line behind the coven. They shiver involuntarily, their pyjamas inadequate against the bitter chill, but it is no matter to the magic users who have summoned them.

Aradia opens her eyes and smiles. 'Shall we?'

The coven begins to stride away down the darkened street, the lamps overhead switching on again one by one behind them as they leave. Their magic now draws the line of children away from their homes, and they follow obediently behind the coven like an juvenile army.

*

Black Annis waits. The human magic users have left her alone, but their spells are strong enough to bind her still. The enchanted pentagram on the ground, in which they have confined her, is powerful — drawn by ritual and imbued with magic. She is confused as to what they have in store. She is certain that their intentions are not good, but their promise of more flesh makes Black Annis salivate in spite of herself.

She decides she must bide her time, allow them to feed her, allow them to facilitate her growing strength. Only then will she act against them, break free of their spell, these foolish, obstinate humans that seem to believe they can influence the tide of the Netherworld.

Black Annis freezes as she hears something overhead, above her in her lair that has now become her prison. Footsteps — so many, some heavy, some light. The scent of the human children hits her like a landslide. Black Annis rises within the confines of the pentagram. Her pale eyes shine brightly. A moment later, the magicians file in, and behind them . . . yes! Black Annis has never seen so many children in one place. She lets out an involuntary growl of eager hunger, but the coven's leader quiets her.

'Patience, crone,' he says, his voice smooth and mocking. He turns to the gathered line of children now standing stiffly beside the other magicians. He walks over to them and places a hand on the head of a fair-haired boy and an oval-faced girl.

'Go to her,' he intones.

The children break out of line and stride towards Black Annis. With a gesture, the coven leader makes a brief passage through the magical barrier that surrounds Black Annis — too brief for her to seize an opportunity to break free. And besides, her hunger for the flesh of these two children is too distracting for her to think of anything else. The girl and boy come to a halt. Their impassive stares register nothing.

Black Annis' own eyes bulge with excitement. A string of blue-black dribble escapes her lips as she creeps

207

forward. Then, using one pointed talon on each of the young humans, Black Annis swiftly stops their hearts, then feverishly sets about removing their skin. She is so overcome with zeal that she allows their pelts to slump to the floor without pausing to spread them out to dry. Black Annis notices from the corner of her luminous eyes that some of the adult humans have turned away. She scoffs — they have not the stomach for their purpose. She will take advantage of their foolishness, and their provisions of food. They have weaknesses, while she grows stronger. Soon, though, they will realise their mistake. She will slay this coven, and the chime child too. Then no one will be able to prevent her from taking her pick of the fragile human children that walk this land.

With no further hesitation, Black Annis tears into each of the skinless bodies, and groans with pleasure as the flesh slides down her throat. And there are so many more to come before she reaches full strength.

Chapter Twenty-Six

'OK, I know I said I wanted you to help, but I'm not sure this is what I had in mind,' Callum said, frowning as Jacob reached one blood-dripping hand towards his shoulder. He could feel the ghostly chill of the Born Dead's hand through his coat as they stood in the churchyard.

'Trust me,' Jacob said, with a glimmer of a smile. Doom looked up at his master expectantly, his red eyes glowing. Jacob put his other hand on Doom's neck and then looked over to Melissa.

'Put your hand on my shoulder,' he said. 'I need to have contact with all of you if I am to attempt this.'

Callum raised his eyebrows. 'Are you sure this is going to work? I don't want to end up a pile of molecules floating around space for the rest of my life. I mean, I know I was complaining about being a chime child, but I'll definitely take it over *that*,' he said, smiling nervously.

Melissa looked a little dubious herself as she placed both hands on Jacob's shoulders. 'Go for it,' she said, squeezing her eyes closed. Callum was about to do the same, when he realised that the world around him had already begun to blur.

It was an unpleasant sensation, like being spun on a turbo-charged fairground ride. Everything was rushing by so dizzyingly that Callum felt sick. He closed his eyes for a moment, hoping to combat the nausea.

When he opened them again, everything was still a dark blur. Slowly he realised that there beside him, in sharp relief among the swirl of dark mist, were Melissa, Jacob and Doom.

And after a moment, all three of them seemed to dissolve into the ether . . .

Then, just as suddenly as the whirling had begun,

Callum felt firm ground underneath his feet. The journey had only lasted seconds, but as the air around him cleared, Callum realised that Jacob really had transported them. Where moments ago they had all been standing in Nether Marlock Churchyard, Callum saw that, although the moon still glowed in night sky above, they were now on what must be the site of Leicester Castle.

'Blimey,' he breathed, rubbing his eyes to make sure he wasn't imagining things. They'd travelled *miles*. He looked over at Jacob, who had stepped away from them and was leaning against a nearby tree to steady himself.

'Jacob, are you OK?' Callum asked. The ghost nodded.

'As I said, my power diminishes the further I get from the churchyard – I feel somewhat drained, that is all.'

'I'm not surprised,' Melissa chimed in. Her face was almost as pale as Jacob's. 'That was *mad*.'

Callum was already looking around at the castle grounds, trying to see if he could locate the entrance that would lead to Black Annis' lair. All that existed of the original eleventh-century castle was the mound upon which it once stood. The soft grass underfoot was crisp with frost, but there was no sign of an entry point for a cave or tunnel. Soon Melissa joined him, scouring the ground and the surrounding areas.

Callum's heart began to pound. What if they were too late? What if his instinct to try and find Annis' lair had been wrong and they were just wasting time? He took a deep breath. There was no time for doubts now – he needed to think.

'I can't see anything,' Melissa called. 'We should have brought torches or something. I guess we'll just have to hope we get lucky.'

As she finished, Callum realised they had something better than a torch.

'Hang on,' he said. 'I have an idea.'

Closing his eyes, Callum held his hands out before him, facing down towards the ground. He turned slowly in a circle and, to his relief, he felt the skin of his hands begin to prickle.

His *Luck* was exactly what they needed. His ability to sense evil . . .

Callum moved his hands back and forth.

Suddenly, as he turned, his fingertips began to tingle madly. He moved to the right a fraction and the feeling faded. Back and to the left – sure enough, the pins and needles intensified. Callum slowly began to move in the direction his hands were driving him.

'Have you found something?' Melissa asked, coming up next to him.

'I might have,' Callum mumbled, concentrating hard.

Melissa turned back to where they had first materialised a short distance away.

'Jacob, do you – Hey, where are Jacob and Doom?' she said suddenly. 'They were there a second ago, now they've vanished.' She turned to Callum with a worried smile. 'You don't think they've abandoned us do you?'

Callum was about to answer her when he heard a shout behind them.

'Excuse me, you two. Just what exactly do you think you're doing here?'

Callum and Melissa both froze, then turned slowly. Callum raised a hand to shield his eyes from the torchlight now being flashed into both their faces.

'Damn,' he whispered.

Melissa glanced at Callum and then raised her voice in the direction of the bright light. 'Uh, we were just, um . . . we're on a dare. Crazy story, but anyway this turned out to be the forfeit for –'

'Spare us, love,' the voice with the torch interrupted. Coming a bit closer, he lowered the light from Callum and Melissa's faces. Callum could see a stocky man in a security guard's uniform and a football scarf striding towards them. A taller, thinner guard walked along next to him. Callum swore silently again under his breath – of all the problems he'd tried to predict, he certainly hadn't counted on a pair of jobsworth patrol men ruining their plans.

But then Callum noticed something was wrong. The two guards were still moving towards them, but their expressions seemed to be changing. From a look of bored sarcasm, the stocky guard's features fell into confusion and concern – and his companion's did the same. Then both men suddenly stopped walking. They seemed rooted to the spot, unable to move, and even in the pale moonlight, Callum could see their faces straining and turning red.

'What are they doing?' Melissa whispered.

Callum shook his head wordlessly. The two men were now visibly quivering in the eerie light of their torches, and their eyes became unfocused. At exactly the same moment, each of the men's eyes rolled up into their sockets so that only the whites showed. Callum stumbled backwards as the shorter, stockier guard raised his hands, still rooted to the spot, his fingers clawing at the air desperately as if imploring Callum and Melissa for help. Callum soon noticed that the other guard was doing the same – and that there were oozing blisters forming all over the men's skin. He reached out instinctively for Melissa's hand and she grabbed it desperately.

'M-Melissa, we should –'

But before Callum could even finish his sentence, his breath was snatched by a gasp of horror. Before their eyes, the stocky man's face split apart in an explosion of blood and grey matter that ripped down the length of his body. Melissa screamed as the body of the second man exploded and a spatter of gore came flying at her. The blasted torsos of the guards stood before them, the remains of their clothing hanging limply in shreds.

Then, to Callum's disbelief, out through the cracked bones and throbbing vital organs of each man clambered a demon the size of a small dog. The monsters' sticklike, hairy arms and legs were cloaked in red flame and, as they escaped the prison of their hosts' ribcages, the demons began to grow. Within seconds they were almost as tall as Callum. The guards' discarded bodies fell to the ground, blood pooling around them on the frost-covered grass.

Callum felt as though everything around him was moving in slow motion. He turned his head and saw Melissa's body crumple to the ground, fainting from shock. In the next instant, he saw one of the hellish demons leap towards Melissa. Red flame illuminated the sky as her body suddenly ignited . . .

Chapter Twenty-Seven

Callum reacted instinctively. Launching himself at Melissa's prone body, he rolled her down the mound they had been standing on and, to his relief, the action smothered the fire. She came to a stop at the bottom, several metres away, conscious again, and gasping with shock and fright.

'Melissa! Are you OK?' Callum shouted, but then he felt the heat of the other demon coming up behind him. He turned to leap out of the way, but the creature's long, bony fingers grabbed him by the hair and hauled him up. Red flames from the demon's hellish hands licked at Callum's hair, igniting it instantly. With a cry, he kicked out at the beast and it released him for a moment. Callum's hands flew up to his head and batted the fire away desperately, but the demon was rounding on him again.

He saw Melissa run for cover near a ruined wall, but his relief was short-lived, as the two fiery creatures stalked towards him, their eerie, orange glow lighting up the night sky. Callum stared at the demons in terror but then he felt something take over: an odd sense of calm . . . and a word beginning to form in his throat.

'NO.'

Callum threw himself at one of the creatures, who now looked like a tangle of hair and flame and evil. It felt like he'd grabbed a bucket of hot coals. The force of Callum's attack knocked the creature into its partner, and Callum rolled away from them, swiping out stray flames, as the two demons scrambled once more to their clawed feet.

Shield, Callum thought . . .

An image of Jacob flying backward in surprise flashed across Callum's brain. He grabbed at the memory, held out his hands, felt the energy flowing from his body.

One of the demons sprang towards him but then faltered.

Back.

Callum threw his entire being into the shield.

As if in slow motion, the demon jerked backwards, pushed relentlessly by the force of Callum's invisible barrier.

BACK.

Callum was determined. For the first time ever, he was fully in control of his power, but he didn't have time to feel pleased; he was focused entirely on the task at hand. Concentrating so hard that he didn't notice the dozens of small burns on his hands and face, Callum forced the evil creature away. But just as he thought he had the upper hand, the second demon leapt at him. Taken by surprise, Callum was forced into a crouch, desperately trying to hold the two creatures off by extending both hands and trying to create a dome of protection with his shield.

Then, out of the corner of his eye, he saw a huge shadow loom over them.

'Doom!' Callum cried. He'd never been more thankful to see the huge, nightmarish dog. With one ferocious snarl, Doom sank his teeth into one of the demons and pulled it off. Callum could see Jacob standing a short distance away with Melissa at his side. She seemed to be saying something, but Callum couldn't quite make it out.

Then he saw it: a tree branch, hovering above the other demon. And, somehow, Melissa was suspending it in the air . . .

It was like a super-charged version of her floating spell with the pencil. Melissa had her hands raised up and, with a sweep of her arms, she sent the branch hurtling down. It smacked into the creature's back, making it howl, then burst into flames as it bounced away.

'Callum, get away!' Melissa shouted. But Callum saw that the demon was distracted, and he seized his opportunity. Flexing his fingers, he almost instantly felt the shift in the power in his palms. Callum raised his hands towards the creature and released the energy that had gathered in them. It slammed into the fiery demon, pulsing around it in bursts. The central core of the bolt seemed to be pinning the demon down on to the ground, while the air around it crackled. The evil creature began to dissolve. It writhed and squealed, but Callum held it fast, the stream of energy from his hands growing broader and stronger as he concentrated. Callum felt a distant thrill of exhilaration, but he didn't let success distract him from finishing the job.

And a moment later, the thing was gone – blown into the ether.

Chapter Twenty-Eight

Callum looked around, breathless and amazed at what he'd achieved. It worked – his power actually worked! He could see Doom still snapping at the other creature, now nothing more than a pile of smoking hair and flesh, before Jacob called him back.

'Nice work with that branch,' Callum said to Melissa, stumbling over to them. 'Are you OK?' He could see that the flames from the demon had singed her clothes a little.

'Yeah, I'm fine – well, relatively speaking. And see, told you I'd come in handy with the old magic!' she said. Callum noticed that her voice was still a little shaky though. Fine was more than Callum could say for his hair – he reached up and felt his head tentatively, but he could tell it wasn't good.

'It'll grow back,' Melissa said sympathetically.

'It's all right,' Callum replied with a smile, 'I was thinking a buzz cut might be more heroic looking anyway.' But as he turned and saw Jacob's grim expression, his own face grew serious.

'Jacob, what just happened? What *were* those things?'

'They were obscura demons. Even I was fooled into thinking that they were ordinary mortals – that is why Doom and I disappeared. But I fear the coven deployed them as guardians in order to protect Black Annis' lair. It is possible to disguise such beasts inside unsuspecting victims using magic.'

'Ugh . . .' Melissa groaned.

'When they detected you were a chime child,' Jacob continued, 'it would have triggered their release.'

'Jeez,' Callum said, disgusted. 'Well, if they've gone to these lengths to guard the area then it seems likely that Annis is here . . . and probably the coven too.'

'Now that their guardians have been disposed of, they

will likely be alerted to our presence,' Jacob replied.

'Then we have to do something *now*,' Callum said. Flexing his fingers, he waited for the tingling to return to his hands so he could try to use it to locate the entrance to Annis' lair again. A short distance away from the castle mound, Callum soon found himself standing over a metal grille, which seemed to lead into unending darkness. He pressed his hands together to stem the aching numbness; he was obviously on to something.

'This must be it,' he called. 'This must lead to the tunnel that will take us to Black Annis. Let's get down there.'

Jacob and Melissa rushed over to his side, but Jacob's face was creased with worry.

'Callum, think for a moment. We must be cautious,' he said, his voice low. For the first time, Callum thought he detected a hint of nerves in the ghost's tone.

'Cautious?' Callum replied incredulously. 'We can't be! We haven't got time for caution, Jacob –'

'You must remember that the strengths of myself and Doom are diminished here. We cannot provide you with the defence we would hope to . . .'

'Doom seemed to do pretty well with that fire-demon thing!' Callum replied.

He reached down and began to pull at the grille, relieved as it came loose in his hands. 'We've got to get down there before . . . before who knows what.'

Callum caught Melissa's anxious stare, but studiously ignored Jacob's gaze as he rattled the grille away. So he was taken completely by surprise when he suddenly felt the chill of Doom's jaws gripping on to the back of his coat.

'What the –? Jacob, call him off . . .'

But Jacob's face was just as determined as Callum's own. Only when the ghost dog had pulled Callum further than arm's reach away from the tunnel entrance did the Born Dead gesture for Doom to release him.

'What are you doing, Jacob?' Callum hissed angrily, trying to keep his voice down. The ghost strode over to him.

'*We* will go in first,' Jacob said, looking over at Doom who was now sitting at his side, his red eyes glowing brightly. 'We must keep you safe until you are needed. Once we have determined that it is secure enough to pass through, you can follow. Melissa, you shall remain above ground and keep watch, alerting us to any movements – any at all.'

Adrenalin was coursing through Callum's veins after the fight with the demons, but he couldn't help thinking grudgingly that perhaps Jacob's suggestion made sense.

'Callum, just let them go in first,' Melissa chimed in. 'If there *is* something else down there guarding the tunnel, maybe Jacob and Doom can deal with it and you'll be free to get to the coven and Black Annis.'

Callum folded his arms, still feeling a stubborn sense of urgency to make something happen himself. Instead he took a deep breath and nodded, although the tingle remained in his hands.

'Fine. Go.'

Jacob looked deep into Callum's eyes. 'We will ensure the path is clear. Once we have determined that, I will whistle – that will be my signal for you to follow.'

'Ghosts can *whistle*?' Melissa asked with a small smile, but Callum remained focused stonily on Jacob as he made his way back towards the opening. Doom jumped down silently and disappeared, blending immediately into the darkness, then Jacob dropped down after him.

'They'd better be quick,' Callum said, looking around him at the eerily silent castle grounds and the shadowy heap of the demon Doom had ripped to shreds. 'I've got a bad feeling about this . . .'

Chapter Twenty-Nine

The dark cave is gripped with an anxious silence as the four human magicians await their leader's return. It has been almost a full day since they last saw sunlight, and the youngest man of the group sniffs the decaying skins of the children they have fed Black Annis, then turns away, his stomach churning. He is eager for their task to be over, and a little resentful that their leader, Varick, has seen fit to come and go at his pleasure while they must wait underground. While before it was enough that Black Annis remained within the enchanted pentagram, now at least two of the coven are required to actively watch over the crone's imprisonment.

'Nolan.'

The younger man turns towards Aradia, who has been keeping watch for the past hour with Maeve, the eldest of their coven.

'Yes, Aradia,' Nolan replies, struggling to keep the sarcasm from his voice. He, like Maeve, grows tired of the power wielded by their leader's second in command.

'You and Gale can take over for now. Leave we women to rest.' Aradia smiles wryly. She knows as much as the younger man does that she is hardly challenged by their current task. Sighing, he and Gale swap places with the women.

'And feed her one more,' Aradia calls over her shoulder as she strides towards the lair's entrance for some fresher air. Nolan gestures, and one more of the children walks towards Black Annis blindly. He grimaces as she pounces upon the boy, stabbing a talon into his chest. There are only five children left. The coven's true task must surely be about to commence. If only they could get this over with, let the real work begin . . .

Suddenly, there is a stirring, a commotion close to the tunnel's entrance into Black Annis' lair. A low, thunderous growl echoes down towards the cave.

'What's going on? Nothing could have got past the obscura demons, surely?' Maeve calls to Aradia, but the flame-haired woman has her arms raised and her face is immoveable with the concentration of weaving a powerful spell. Her fingers flex and bend at an impossible speed, her lips moving fast, her words incomprehensible. The elder woman turns to her fellow coven members and shouts.

'There's movement in the tunnel, be on your guard.'

Maeve rushes towards the entrance, but Aradia is already pulling something through the passageway and into the lair using her magic. She draws in two iron cages, woven with magic. And inside the cages are two ghosts: one, a Born Dead spirit, the other an enormous black dog – a Churchyard Grim – whose giant frame is hunched in the confines of the metal prison. At last, Aradia lowers her hands, her shoulders heaving with the effort of the spell she has executed.

'Well, well, well,' she says between breaths. 'What do we have here?'

Chapter Thirty

Callum and Melissa waited silently and anxiously by the opening, straining their ears for Jacob's signal. It had been at least ten minutes since he had gone into the tunnel with Doom. Callum could feel his stomach turning into knots, and his hands were burning with the sensation that told him something was definitely wrong. He glanced fretfully behind him every few seconds, worried that there might be more demons sent by the coven to guard the lair's entrance.

'What's that?' Melissa gasped, as a high, keening noise pierced the silent night. They both stopped breathing for a moment, before Callum realised it was an ambulance siren. He exhaled and swallowed hard.

'Something's up,' he said. 'It's been way too long.'

He looked over at Melissa and she nodded, her face pale with concern.

'What should we do?'

Callum paused for a moment, looking around into the darkness. He turned back to Melissa.

'We're going to go down there.'

'We?' Melissa looked unsure. 'Jacob said that I should stay up here in case . . .'

'Melissa, I don't think it's any more dangerous down there than it is up here. We don't know what's going on. I think it's better for us to stick together,' he said. 'Besides, your skills could come in handy, remember?'

Melissa smiled shakily. 'OK then – let's do it.'

Taking a deep breath, Callum hoisted himself over the grille, then let go and dropped down into the darkness. He had no idea how far he'd fall, but thankfully it was only a couple of metres.

'Callum?' He heard Melissa's voice above him.

'It's OK, it's not far – I'll help you,' he breathed, hoping she'd hear him.

The blackness was virtually absolute, and Callum could almost hear his heart thumping through his chest. He could just about make out Melissa's boots dangling above him, and a moment later she dropped down beside him. She jumped as Callum reached out to grab her arm.

'Do you have your phone?' he whispered.

'Who are you planning to call, the Paranormal Police?' she said through shaky breaths. Callum couldn't help a nervous chuckle.

'Just hand it over,' he said, and he felt around in the darkness until his hand connected with Melissa's and she passed him her mobile phone. Callum pressed at the buttons until the screen illuminated, and finally they could just about see each other.

'Ah, good thinking,' Melissa said, her tentative smile shadowed by the weak light of the phone.

'Come on,' Callum urged, and they began to inch their way into the dank catacombs beneath the ruins of Leicester Castle. The musty smell of the tunnel was overpowering. Other than the dull echo of their footsteps and their nervous breathing, it was almost *deathly* quiet. Callum shivered; it couldn't be a good sign.

But just as the thought entered Callum's head, he heard voices – they were very faint, some distance away, but they were definitely there. He reached out and held up his hand for Melissa to wait. They both held their breath and listened hard. Callum couldn't make out exactly what was being said, but he could tell that none of the voices was Jacob's. His mouth went dry as he finally made out one phrase.

'. . . Born Dead . . .' Then a few more muffled words and subdued laughter.

'Do you think it's the coven?' Melissa whispered, but Callum held his finger up to his mouth to quiet her. He nodded silently and Melissa's eyes widened, then her brow furrowed determinedly. She gestured that they should keep going.

Callum nodded once more and took a deep breath. Holding the phone above their heads, he began to cdge forward through the tunnel again, with Melissa following close behind. They moved so slowly it seemed they'd barely gone a few steps before Callum stopped suddenly when the tunnel went dark. He felt Melissa bump into his back, and she took in a sharp, frightened breath.

'Sorry,' he murmured, pressing again at the buttons of the phone and holding it up. As the screen lit up once more, Callum recoiled in horror, holding out his arm to stop Melissa.

The passage ahead was littered with bones.

There was no doubt that the debris was human – more than likely the grisly remains of Black Annis' recent kills, Callum thought. All around them, he now noticed scatterings of child-sized ribs and limbs. Two small skulls lay side by side on the floor ahead.

Melissa's hands flew up to her mouth.

Callum swallowed hard, and his fingers suddenly went ice cold.

He froze as he was hit by a flashing vision of himself, one foot ensnared in the cage-like bones of a dead child's ribs in the passage ahead of them.

The bones were a trap.

Callum's foot hovered precariously in the air, but before he could stop her, Melissa kept moving, pushing into him.

'Come on, Callum,' she insisted. 'It's disgusting, but we can't stop now, we have to find Jacob and Doom, and –'

'Melissa!' Callum yelled, forgetting to be quiet. 'Don't!'

But it was too late. His echoing voice reverberated around them and, one second later, his foot landed in the middle of one of the rib cages.

It snapped shut around his ankle.

Chapter Thirty-One

Melissa gave Callum a desperate look. Without thinking, she stepped towards him, and Callum's heart sank as a trap snapped shut around her ankle too. He found he couldn't move a muscle; the bones were somehow keeping them both frozen to the spot. Try as he might, Callum couldn't pull himself free of the supernatural trap. He could see that his friend was beginning to mutter something intently under her breath.

'Melissa? What are you doing?' he hissed.

The bones around her foot began to twitch and Callum's eyes widened hopefully. She seemed to be trying to counter the magic that was holding them. But Melissa was cut short as they saw a light in the tunnel ahead of them begin to grow brighter.

Someone was coming.

Footsteps grew louder, and a pair of shadows began to loom around a bend in the tunnel. Callum's heart quickened. Finally he saw two women approaching them. He struggled to free himself, but it was hopeless. Soon the two women were in front of them.

'Who are you?' one of them asked. She was tall and willowy and, in the flickering light of the flaming torch she was carrying, Callum could tell that she had long red hair. He remained stonily silent, but the woman had now turned to Melissa and was eyeing her closely.

'A magic user – I sense it. Foolish girl, to think you could undo this spell.' The woman turned back to Callum and held her hand in front of him, as though trying to detect something.

'Hmm,' she muttered. 'But in you, young man, I do not sense the same sort of power. What brings you here, if you –' She broke off suddenly and raised her eyebrows in realisation. 'Goodness me, who would have thought?'

She turned to her elder female companion and laughed, the mockingly melodic sound of it bouncing off the walls of the tunnel.

'Maeve, I think what we have here is the last of the *chime children*!'

She made a sweeping gesture with her hands. Callum and Melissa's arms were suddenly pinned to their sides. Callum struggled desperately to try and manifest the power that was building furiously in his hands, but it was no use. His hands remained flat against his legs. A moment later, the traps around their feet fell open, and Callum felt himself being dragged off the ground and up into the air.

'No – stop!' he said through gritted teeth, but the woman just smiled slowly.

Moving his eyes to the side as much as he could, Callum saw the same thing happening to Melissa. She let out a cry and he could see her trying to blink back tears of frustration. They were being pulled through the air by the women's magic, through the tunnel towards the lair.

In the pale light, Callum could tell that many of the bones scattered down the length of the tunnel were still fresh, with scraps of flesh still attached and teeth marks evident. It was grotesque and sickening, but Callum forced himself to keep his eyes open. He had to be aware of what was happening, wait for any chance to break free.

The passage now opened abruptly into a cave. At last they had reached Black Annis' lair.

Callum surveyed the scene in horror.

A pair of pale glowing orbs slowly became visible in the murkiness of the cavern. They were Black Annis' eyes, the sickly luminescent green of decay. Strewn around her feet were the partially eaten corpses of half a dozen children, surrounded by a large, elaborate pentagram drawn on the dusty floor in what Callum was almost certain was blood. Two men stood on either side of it, holding their arms slightly away from their bodies with their eyes closed. It looked as though they were somehow keeping the prison intact.

As Callum's eyes searched further, he was shocked to see a small group of children standing in one corner of the cave. They were still alive, but their eyes were glazed and their bodies stiff. They gazed unseeing into the darkness, obviously under some kind of spell too. Callum suddenly remembered his earlier vision of a kid wandering to the front door like a zombie. He cursed silently.

And then, finally, Callum's eyes came to rest on those of Jacob. He swallowed hard as he saw the Born Dead and Doom caged in separate iron prisons. Jacob's black eyes were narrowed with a hard, pained stare, and Doom began to emit a relentless, otherworldly whine.

Callum finally felt his feet touch the ground, though he and Melissa remained frozen by the women's invisible magic.

'Oh, poor little ghosts – they don't seem to like iron very much,' the red-headed woman cooed. Callum's mind darted back to a conversation he'd once had with Jacob, in which the Born Dead had mentioned that iron could be used as a ward against Netherworld beings. He clenched his jaw and spoke.

'What the hell are you doing?' Callum snarled.

'Don't you worry yourself with the details, chime child,' the red-headed woman retorted. 'Suffice it to say that your feeble attempts to thwart our plan have proved futile. What did you expect – that you, one little chime child, and your pathetic band of friends would be able to stop us?'

'Aradia,' the older woman said, interrupting. 'We don't have much time before Varick returns. We should get rid of them.'

Callum's heart quickened as the woman called Aradia stepped towards him. Her face threateningly close to his own, she answered the older coven member.

'And just *what*, my dear Maeve, do you propose we do with them?'

The white-haired woman paused, and then her face twisted into a callous grin.

'We should feed them to the hag.'

Chapter Thirty-Two

'NO!' Melissa's shout was so loud and determined that for a moment, even the entranced children seemed to stir, before their staring eyes glazed over once more.

'Shhh,' Aradia hissed, mockingly. 'Don't worry, sweetheart. There's no need to get yourself all worked up now, is there?' She turned to Maeve with a frown.

'And *you* – don't be so hasty. They could be useful; they have some power, they could be turned. Either way, soon we will begin, and their efforts to stop us will be less than nothing.'

Callum could hear Melissa sigh with tentative relief, though he was still unable to turn his body to look at her and give her any sign of encouragement. He could feel rage and frustration boiling inside him.

'Besides,' Aradia continued, moving back over to Melissa, 'perhaps you, my girl, might want to follow in my footsteps? You would be far better served using your magic to side with those who will soon wield all the power –'

'Never in a million *years*,' Melissa spat, regaining her voice, but Aradia merely emitted her tinkling laugh once more.

'You may well have your wish when we sacrifice this crone and the crossing point is made wide enough for the Demon Lord to enter the mortal world. Then our rule shall last a million years and more. Those who do not surrender to us will be doomed. Think carefully. You could thrive under my guidance.'

'She might need guidance, but definitely not from *you*,' Callum said through gritted teeth.

'Chime child,' Aradia scoffed. 'Pathetic does not begin to describe your attempt to stop what's about to happen. You should be ashamed of yourself – you're an insult to your kind. I think keeping you alive for the Demon Lord to deal with will be a nice opener. Brace yourself – you'll have a front-row seat to a future blacker than you can ever imagine.'

'Enough!' came a shout from behind them.

Aradia whirled around angrily, but Maeve held her ground.

'*Enough*, Aradia. We must prepare. We do not have time to waste.'

Frowning, the younger woman turned away from Callum and Melissa.

'Fine,' she snarled. 'Let's get on with it.'

All four of the magic users gathered beside the pentagram now, their heads dipped, talking quickly in low voices. Callum felt anger and desperation welling up inside him. He squeezed his eyes shut and put all his will into trying to break free of Aradia's spell, but it was no use. He could hardly move.

But as he opened his eyes, he saw someone else struggling to free themselves – and it wasn't Melissa. To his amazement, Black Annis seemed to be moving her clawed fingers and muttering to herself. Was she trying to use her own magic against the coven's? Her fingers worked back and forth, unnoticed by her captors, her claws rustling the nightmarish skirts of dried skin around her legs.

Suddenly, Callum had a thought.

Summoning all his strength, he desperately tried to move, grunting with the effort. With the coven's attentions elsewhere for a moment, it seemed the spell binding him was becoming fractionally weaker and, sweating hard, Callum finally managed to raise his hands just enough for his palms to face down towards the ground. He focused all the energy that had been boiling over inside him and, with a final growl, he forced it downwards through his hands. The energy rippled along the floor of the cave towards the pentagram that enclosed Black Annis – and just as Callum had hoped, its force was enough to disrupt its form. The movement seemed to have taken the coven by surprise – and, for all her skill, Aradia's binding magic seemed to be disrupted by Callum's energy bolt.

It was all he needed.

Callum grabbed Melissa's arm and pulled her to one side, out of the coven's line of sight.

'Callum, how did you – ?' Melissa began, but she was silenced as she realised what Callum had already seen, what he'd already hoped for . . .

Black Annis was loose.

Furious, Aradia screamed a spell and flung her hands out towards the hag. To Callum's amazement, she had conjured a ball of crackling energy like sparks of lightning, and she flung it out at the crone. But Callum could see that their feedings had already taken effect; Black Annis was now strong. *Very* strong.

Black Annis dodged, her stringy hair flying out behind her as Aradia bowled another ball of lightning at the hag, fast and furious. This one caught Annis' arm and set the rags of her dress blazing. She spat blue-black saliva on the fire to put it out and deflected the next of Aradia's attacks with a flick of her talons. She sent the sparking missile straight back, but Aradia managed to move out of the way just in time. Instead, it caught Nolan by surprise, smashing into him and igniting his clothes instantly.

He cried out in pain as Aradia rallied, and the two older coven members fell in alongside her. They chanted in a loud, unfamiliar language that seemed to create a whirlwind around the cave. The cone of spinning air whipped towards Black Annis, but she bared her black teeth in a cackle.

Her talons already glowed red-hot where Aradia's balls of lightning had touched them. Now the light in her long nails grew more intense. Black Annis held out her hands toward the whirlwind, her fingers spread wide, and slashed at the air, breaking the spell effortlessly. Without pausing, she launched herself towards the three magicians, still clawing. Her talons caught the torso of Maeve, digging furiously into her shoulder and back as she turned to try and escape the onslaught.

With a cry of pain, the white-haired woman fled towards the tunnel that led above ground, and Callum could see that the two other coven men were following close behind her.

Aradia, on the other hand, was standing her ground. With a furious cry, she launched another attack at Black Annis, sending a huge, crackling ball of energy towards the demon.

Callum thought it might have been too much for Annis, but with her new strength, she was once again too fast. Black Annis raised both of her taloned hands and deflected the blast – but this time it flew straight towards where Callum and Melissa were crouched . . .

'Callum!' Melissa cried out.

Without hesitation, Callum knocked Melissa sideways out of the path of the ball of energy. Feeling an eerie sense of calm, he braced himself for the impact of the blast, covering his head with his hands, his palms facing outwards as he threw up his shield. Aradia seemed to have put absolutely every bit of energy she had into creating the huge sphere. But this time Callum wasn't going to be taken off guard.

The jolt came, throwing him against the cave wall and knocking the air from his lungs. The bolt of energy crackled up and down his body; Callum's flesh prickled with electricity, as though thousands of needles were brushing him from head to toe. It was ferocious, but not painful. His breath came back to him in choking gasps and he blinked hard.

For a moment, a stillness seemed to descend on the

cave, but as the dust settled Callum saw Black Annis bare her black teeth in a snarl. Before Callum could blink, she launched herself towards Aradia with an otherworldly screech, pouncing on top of the red-headed woman and sinking her teeth into her neck.

Aradia screamed in pain, but managed to wrench herself free and send one last blast of electrical energy at the crone. It was clear that the magician was weak, but it was enough to force Black Annis away from her. The demon recoiled, and Callum watched with a mixture of anger and disgust as Aradia turned and ran towards the tunnel, clutching her neck as blood began to seep between her fingers. A moment later, she was gone.

Black Annis turned slowly towards Callum.

Chapter Thirty-Three

'*You*, chime child,' Black Annis spat, her voice rasping and cruel. 'You leave me to do your work – to thwart these pathetic human magicians who seek to destroy me?'

Callum balled his hands into fists, ready for any sudden attack. 'I think it worked out pretty well, actually,' he snarled back.

With a furious cry, Black Annis flashed through the air with super-human speed and slashed her claws at him. There was so much strength behind the strike that Callum almost felt his bones rattle. But instead of cutting into him, Black Annis' talons ricocheted off his invisible shield.

'Callum!'

It was Jacob's bell-like voice, firmly calling out his name.

'Remember your powers, all your training – you are able to resist her. Do not fear her magic.'

Callum turned his head toward the iron cage the coven had built around the ghost. Cringing away from the touch of the iron bars, Jacob was coming to his aid in the only way he could now: as a guide, as a teacher.

Callum nodded, his breath coming out in bursts as he struggled to maintain his shield against the demon's slashing, gnarled hands. With an enormous effort he thrust the barrier forward, forcing Black Annis to scuttle backwards on her clawed, bare blue feet. Another push of the barrier and she skidded across the floor, crashing into the bars of the cage in which Doom was enclosed. Recoiling from the iron and Doom's snapping jaws, Black Annis rounded on Callum.

'Fool!' she snarled. She raised her hands once more, and with a burst of power, launched another onslaught, her claws tearing at the shield with all her might. Callum's barrier kept her talons from breaking through, but he felt a rising sense of panic as his entire body tingled with the relentlessness of Black Annis' attack. Although she couldn't injure him, she was forcing him backwards again and he'd soon be trapped.

Then, out of the corner of his eye, Callum saw Melissa move out from the shadows where she'd been hiding from the fight, clutching something in her hand. Before he could shout for her to stop, Melissa ran straight at Black Annis and flung a handful of dirt from the cave floor at the crone's glowing eyes. She whispered something quickly under her breath and the dirt seemed to balloon, enveloping the demon in a cloud of dust.

She'd taken Black Annis by surprise, but the hag flailed her arms, enraged, swiping blindly with her claws. Melissa cried out and stumbled away, and Callum saw gashes all along one side of her face dripping thick blood.

That was all it took.

Callum threw himself forwards, feeling the anger

and determination building inside him until his hands burned with the energy he was about to release. He burst through the cloud of dust towards Black Annis with a grimace that almost matched the crone's own. Pushing his hands together he put all his being into creating a blast of power like the one he had used on that fateful day in the alleyway. He felt the energy flowing through his hands, making the air around them shimmer and crackle.

And this time, Callum hit his mark.

The ripples of power slammed straight into Black Annis' chest and she went flying backwards, smashing into the other side of the cave. She fell into a heap and groaned, shaking her head from side to side as she tried to recover from the blast. For a second Callum thought it was over. But as he watched, the crumpled figure gave a shudder. His eyes widened as Black Annis gathered herself off the hard ground. She found her feet, hunched, crouched and then tensed for a leap. The power in her legs was incredible, and the dead skins of her skirt slapped against her blue flesh. She sailed five feet into the air, talons outstretched, ready to tear and strip. Callum threw his hands out towards her once more, and another blast of energy sent the hag hurtling backwards. This time he refused to relent, putting every ounce of his being into it and holding the beam steadily on her. It pinned the demon to the ground, and she hissed, snapping her putrid teeth, writhing and wriggling in her attempts to get free.

Callum closed in on the demon, taking the initiative as his powers began to take their toll. Reaching her quivering body, he bent down and grabbed Black Annis by her thin blue ankles. She went rigid with pain as the energy radiated out of his fingertips with a crackle and fizz. The hag cried out in anguish, spraying flecks of blue-black spittle, and Callum swallowed bile as his hands brushed against the skins at the edge of her skirt. But he held on, his palms firm against the crone's flesh. Ripples of power flowed from him and spread across her body.

'Callum, be careful!' Melissa cried out from behind him, but her voice sounded muffled through the ringing in his ears.

With a strangled growl, he sent another wave of energy rippling over Black Annis' body. With the last of her strength, she let out a terrible grating shriek. She twisted this way and that, kicking out at Callum violently, but he refused to let go. He dodged to avoid getting a razor-sharp toenail in the eye, and he could feel sweat pouring off him with the effort of keeping her down . . . but then he saw it.

Smoke.

The energy from his hands seemed to be causing Black Annis' blue flesh to combust. The dried skins of the hag's skirt began to singe and burn. Callum choked, but he didn't let go. In that instant, the swell of power burst from his hands in a blaze of blue-white flame as pure as starlight. Wave upon wave of power surged through Callum's hands. The energy ignited a raging blue blaze that roared like flames in a chimney around Black Annis' body. The fire engulfed the crone, and Callum pulled his hands away, standing up he let his arms drop to his sides in exhaustion. His work was done. The blaze raged out of control, and he stumbled back and away from the demon, his eyes wide with amazement.

From amongst the flames, Black Annis let out one last, inhuman screech that made the hairs on Callum's neck stand up.

Then she was gone.

For a few long seconds a cloud of ash swirled around the cave, then settled gently to the ground in a harmless heap, like the sand at the bottom of an hourglass.

Black Annis had finally come to rest in her lair.

Chapter Thirty-Four

Callum ran to Melissa's side. She was crouched on the floor looking stunned. One hand was clutching her cheek, and blood seeped in between her fingers. Callum could feel the power still springing from his own fingertips, but this time his intention was to heal. He laid his hand gently against the torn skin at Melissa's temple and along the side of her cheek, making her wince. Then slowly, deliberately, Callum used the energy radiating from his palm to begin sealing the slashes on his friend's face.

'Does that hurt?' Callum asked.

'It stings! Like antiseptic.' She grinned at him

weakly. 'How do I look?'

Callum laughed and said confidently, 'If you can stand it for a few more seconds, there won't be any scars.'

Melissa nodded and, sure enough, a few moments later she ran her hand over her smooth cheek. 'Excellent work, Dr Scott,' she said with a shaky smile. 'If the whole chime child thing doesn't work out, I hear there's good money in plastic surgery.'

Callum helped Melissa to her feet. She rushed over to the group of children who were gradually becoming more aware of their surroundings as the coven's spell started to wear off. They began to back away and cower in the corner, clearly terrified. Callum went over to Jacob and Doom. To his relief, the spell that had created the iron cages had also now dissipated, and the Born Dead stood calmly while Doom went to guard the entrance to the cave. The Grim's red eyes glowed and his white fangs were bared and shining in his shadowy muzzle.

'Impressive, chime child,' Jacob said. 'You have proven yourself worthy of the title indeed.'

Callum smiled tightly, feeling utterly spent after everything they had faced. 'I couldn't stop them from escaping though.'

'Nonsense,' Jacob said, looking Callum dead in the eye. 'Your task was to defeat Black Annis before the humans could sacrifice her and bring on the full force of the Shadowing. You have succeeded in just that.'

Melissa walked over to them, her face serious.

'They want to get out of here,' she said, glancing over her shoulder at the children, most of whom were weeping uncontrollably.

'Doom,' Jacob said quietly, and the Grim moved aside. The children ran blindly down the tunnel from the cave before Callum or Melissa could stop them.

'They will be all right,' Jacob said. 'The authorities will find them and they will be back safely with their families very soon. It is best if you are not involved in their discovery; the fewer questions you must answer, the better.'

Callum nodded grudgingly, but Melissa shook her head.

'I'll ring the police,' she said, pointing to Callum's pocket, which still held her mobile phone. 'It can be anonymous.'

'Come on then,' Callum said. 'Let's get out of here.'

Doom bounded ahead of them, his red eyes glowing in the dark, but then he gave a sudden, urgent snarl that caused all of them to stop. The ghost dog growled, sniffing the air in the foul tunnel. Then he gave an echoing bark at something hidden in the murky darkness ahead of them.

They froze as a deep voice called out. 'Who is there?'

Cold shuddered down Callum's back. In the blackness of the underground tunnel a small flame appeared. Its eerie violet glow slowly advancing towards them. After a moment Callum saw that it was dancing on the palm of a hand held below a human face – a man's face, handsome and world-weary, neither young nor old. The face, lit by the flame on the man's palm, was frowning and quizzical. Callum swallowed and took a determined step forward, his fists clenched, the last of his power still ready to be released.

'Who are you?'

The man glared sharply at Callum and his companions. A look of surprise seemed to spread across his features, before he composed them once more.

'Chime child? The final of your kind,' the man breathed and then he cleared his throat. 'I am impressed. But you must know that you're well out of your depth in this place.'

'Who *are* you?' Callum repeated with angry urgency. 'Are you their leader? Are you that coven scum's leader? They said you were coming back. Well, guess what? You're a bit late to the party.' He could feel his hands prickle with energy begging to be released.

'Callum,' Jacob began, his voice sounding concerned, cautionary.

'I sense you feel some misplaced glory?' the man interrupted, his voice cold. 'You should know, chime child, that my coven will not be defeated.'

'Black Annis is dead,' Callum said, his fingernails digging into his burning palms. 'So you're out of luck. You're insane, thinking you could bring some demon lord over here.'

The man laughed a callous, short laugh, and stared at Callum with unreadable eyes. The flame in his palm reflected in them menacingly. He ignored Callum's question, but his voice took up a mocking tone. 'Oh? What's that? Killed the hag *yourself*, did you? But you're not quite as proud of it as you should be, are you? You still feel like a failure, don't you boy?'

Callum frowned, confused – there was something about the way the man spoke that felt as though he was getting strangely close to the truth.

'No . . . No, there's not much to be proud of, is there?' the stranger continued to probe. 'A loner, and miserable about it. No one understands you. The weight of the world on your shoulders, and you're not up to any of the tasks being set for you –'

'You don't know what you're talking about,' Callum snarled.

'The truth hurts, doesn't it? *If only you could talk to your mother* . . . Ah! If only you could talk to your mother about it, Mummy would know what to do –'

With wave of shock, Callum realised that the man was reading his mind. He had fixed his eyes on

Callum's face, but could somehow see straight through him.

'SHUT UP!' Callum cried out in fury. Melissa grabbed her friend's arms to hold him back.

'Yes, you'd like to see your mother again, wouldn't you? But she's –'

The man stopped suddenly, mid-sentence, as though something had interrupted his train of thought, but before he could speak again, Jacob stepped in front of Callum.

Now the man's face registered a different kind of surprise.

'Jacob?'

Jacob bowed his head in his characteristic, old-fashioned greeting.

'So,' the mind-reader snarled. 'Making new friends, I see?'

Jacob growled a single word.

'Doom.'

Doom lunged toward the stranger.

But before Doom's snapping jaws could make contact, the violet flame in the man's palm went out. He had simply vanished. Doom sailed through empty air and landed in shadow on the bare floor of the tunnel.

'Where is he?' Callum shouted. 'Where did he go?'

They all looked around, baffled, but there was nothing. Jacob turned to the others quickly. 'We must go.'

Doom shepherded Callum and Melissa up the tunnel, but they didn't need telling twice. Soon they were up through the passage and out into the icy cold night air.

'What was that about? Who *was* that?' Melissa asked, panting. Callum, still reeling with the shock of having his mind invaded and his deepest secrets stripped bare, remained silent.

Jacob paused for a moment. 'Callum, I am sorry. I did not realise at first what he was doing, or I would have interrupted him sooner.'

'Who was he, Jacob?' Callum said finally, turning and glaring at ghost boy. 'How did he know who you were?'

'He is a powerful magic-user,' Jacob said carefully. 'One whose path crossed with my own many years ago. I should have known it might be him who was behind this.'

'You knew this guy before?' Callum folded his arms, frowning hard. 'What did he mean, "making new friends?"'

Jacob was silent for a moment. He turned away from Callum's inquiring gaze to watch Doom stalk back to his side before speaking again. 'When I first knew that man, he was not . . . as he is now. He has been corrupted, much as I have warned that you could be, if you do not tread carefully. We must be extremely vigilant now. Our enemies are close. Closer than we could have imagined.'

Callum shook his head at the ghost's cryptic answers. He sighed, his breath pluming in the starlit night. He'd had enough of questions for now.

'I just want to get home,' Melissa said, echoing Callum's thoughts.

Callum didn't even have time to say anything more before he felt Jacob's cold hand on his shoulder, and the grey mist swirling around them.

Moments later, they were all back in Marlock

Wood, standing with Doom among the familiar tombstones of the churchyard. Callum looked at each of his companions, and he knew their solemn faces reflected his own.

There seemed to be secrets, mysteries and conspiracies around every corner. Callum's mind was whirling with a million questions. How could there be people, *humans*, who were willing to sacrifice everything good about the world for their own selfish gain? How far were they willing to go? No matter how hard Callum had *thought* dealing with the Shadowing would be, it was turning out to be ten times harder.

'You should both be on your way.' Jacob's voice broke the silence. Callum nodded.

'Come on, Melissa,' he said. His friend looked pale and tired. 'Let's go.'

They began to make their way out of the churchyard when Jacob spoke once more.

'Callum,' he said. Callum stopped and turned around. 'Well done.'

Callum looked at the Born Dead's solemn face and smiled.

'See you soon, Jacob.'

The ghost boy remained still, looking at the chime child for a moment, and then turned away. Callum glanced at Melissa and shrugged, then the two of them began to walk along the path and out of the churchyard.

'What do you think will happen now?' Melissa asked quietly.

Callum looked over at her and set his jaw determinedly.

'I don't know exactly what we're going to have to face. I may not be able to protect the entire Boundary. But my powers are getting better; yours are too. And there's one thing I know we *can* focus on.' He paused. 'The coven. We're going to stop them.'

Epilogue

In the dark, echoing space, Varick waits alone. He is hesitant, anxious. He swallows hard and clenches his fist for a moment before snapping his fingers and igniting a flame. He drops it down into the centre of the room and the fire catches, creating violet flames that cast an unearthly light around the walls. The crystal on his finger glows blinding white. He is not a coward, but as his master's terrifying face looms into view among the flames, his heart quickens.

'Tell me,' commands the demon with a hiss.

'Black Annis is destroyed,' the man says bleakly. 'We were unable to use her in our sacrifice.' He closes his eyes and looks away from the demon's inevitable fury. He takes a deep breath as the hideous face flickers in the flames. Its slitted, goat-like pupils are narrow with anger.

'How?' the spitting voice demands. 'Look at me, mortal, and explain your failure.'

'The last chime child,' the man admits, his own voice low. Reluctantly, he looks up at the demon, as commanded. In its fury the demon's eyes blaze crimson. The violet flames sizzle and snap.

'The *sole* chime child thwarted you and your coven?' the demon screeches. 'How can this be?'

'I warned you of this,' the magician replies grimly. 'One chime child is still one guardian for the Boundary, and this youth is invested with tremendous power. He does not even realise its full extent yet. And he has some formidable allies, it seems.'

'You *must* seek him out. He cannot be allowed to remain.' The demon's voice crackles.

'I know where I can find him,' the man says through his teeth. He pauses and frowns, before a cruel smile forms on his lips. 'But to bring about his defeat we must be certain of success. The child has a weakness. One that can be exploited.'

The demon's smile is crueller than the man's, and uglier. 'Go on,' the hideous mouth spits.

'I've seen deep into the boy's heart. He's strong and determined. But he has one fatal flaw. In the right circumstances, I am certain he could be tempted.'

The demon chuckles. Its laughter is like an avalanche of falling rocks. It is no longer angry. It is scheming anew.

'Yessss,' it hisses. 'But you must be more than certain, mortal. You must make good on our agreement, or you will face the consequences when the Shadowing reaches its zenith.'

'I will not let you down,' the man says. A moment later, the flames are extinguished and the space is plunged into darkness once more. He waits in the silence for a moment.

'Varick?'

The voice startles him, but then he realises who it is.

'Aradia,' he says, his voice grim. 'You failed me.'

The woman emerges from the shadows and steps

towards him. He can see that she has been injured, but he maintains a stony glare.

'We shall not fail again, Varick. I promise you that,' she says, her eyes narrowed venomously at the memory of defeat.

'The coven remains intact?'

'It does,' she replies. 'And we are ready for instruction.'

The man smiles, his voice now little more than a whisper.

'I know exactly what must be done . . .'

Turn over if you dare for a chilling preview of the third book in the series . . .

THE SHADOWING
DOOMED

It is the dead of night in the dead of winter. Thick cloud hangs in the black sky, reflecting the dull glow of the sleeping city. Above the ice of the frozen River Mersey, three red lights dance; pinpoints of brightness in the dark.

The Will o' the Wisp is following the river towards the point where it has been called. It has been summoned by a new master.

The Wisp's red lights flit together along the cold, hard surface of the river, but come to a halt as they reach the towering arches of the Stockport Viaduct. Beneath one of the tall tunnels of Victorian brick slumps a human youth. A young creature — a runaway, far from home.

An irresistible opportunity.

The Wisp floats towards the shivering boy. It cannot help itself. Its Master's call can wait a while . . .

*

He doesn't know what makes him open his eyes.

The boy had just begun to drift into a fretful sleep, but now he wakes and looks up. Before him is the most beautiful sight he's ever seen. He forgets cold, forgets hunger, forgets how miserable he is. He simply stares in amazement as three red lights float up to him and quietly bob and weave around his shoulders. They're like tiny, playful stars, red and bright. He blinks, scarcely able to believe it. What are they . . .? Where have they come from? And –

'Follow us . . .'

'Come on . . .'

'Come with us . . .'

The words are no louder than a whisper. The lights . . . they're speaking to him. Somehow, their voices are like the sweetest music he's ever heard.

They want him to go after them . . . he must go with them . . .

The boy staggers to his feet. The lights dart away from him, and then pause.

He steps towards them.

*

The Wisp tumbles over itself in glee. The weak human is slipping into its thrall.

From the top of the viaduct, the still night is pierced with the distant wail of a train's horn. Behind a barbed-wire fence, a series of caged iron ladders lead up to the tracks. Yes — the perfect place. This is where they will go.

The Wisp fights to control its bubbling anticipation. Its three red lights dance eagerly through the links of the fence and hover for a moment, weaving between one ladder's iron rungs. The metal would be a threat to some from the Netherworld, but it feels no ill effect.

The human trudges, entranced, towards the fence. The Wisp has him now.

He will follow.

*

The boy begins to climb the fence without thinking. When he reaches the length of barbed wire, he sinks his palms into the sharp prongs of metal, and does not flinch as they tear open the flesh of his hands and rip his jeans. None of that matters. The glowing red stars light the handholds for him. It's so easy.

'Come up . . .'

'Yes . . .'

'Up here . . .'

The boy's hands slip a little on the rungs of the ladder as thick blood seeps from his wounds, but he holds his grip. The climb is over before he even realises it. He clambers over the guardrail, and he's at the top of the huge viaduct, high as he's ever been, with all the twinkling city's lamps spread out in the darkness below him. The red lights dance along the tracks, lighting the steel with their glow. He feels no fear, only exhilaration.

'Follow . . .'

'Follow . . .'

'Follow us . . .'

The dancing lights lead him along the humming rails.

*

The Wisp has forgotten the true purpose of its journey along the river. For the moment, its whole being knows nothing more than the compulsion to lure this boy. The sheer delight of its imminent success sends the Wisps' lights into a tumbling, whirling frenzy.

The train tracks begin to rattle and vibrate loudly.

Ahead of the stumbling boy, the sound of the approaching train is building to a roar. The three lights dance in the space between the speeding metal missile and the helpless human. The moment is close, so very close. The boy has no hope . . .

*

The boy steps forward lightly, one foot and then the other, balancing along a trembling metal rail. Carefree. Nothing can stop him. The lights are so *beautiful.*

They dart and loop like fireflies before his eyes . . .

But then, behind them, suddenly making their lovely gleam seem dull, a new light builds. White and blinding in its brightness.

As it thunders nearer, the red lights shoot upwards into the dark sky like exploding fireworks. The boy is confused for a moment. Where are they going? He wants them to stay; he wants them to come back . . .

In the blink of an eye, the three lights disappear altogether.

The boy stops for a moment. He frowns and looks around, confused. Where is he? The wind buffets him this way and that – he's high up somewhere. How did he get there? And that noise, that terrible noise is getting louder and louder. He can hardly see. He throws a hand up to shield his face, but the wall of white is blinding him, and he can't understand what's happening.

A train's horn blasts.

A shot of dread pierces through to the boy's core. But it's too late. The world is filled with light and noise – the blaring horn, the scream of steel, the screeching brakes.

The boy squeezes his eyes shut.

A moment later, there is silence.

*

Above the tons of thundering metal that have now ground to a halt, above the pulped wreck of the human body beneath it, the Will o' the Wisp's lights dance contentedly. Its compulsion is satisfied once more. For now, at least . . .

Then its attention is caught — arrested — by a shadowy figure standing on the riverbank below.

Its Master is here.

Another human — but not a weakling to be toyed with like the pathetic creature the Wisp has just led to his doom. No, this human is a man of strength, a magician who wields the dark power of the Netherworld and bends it to his command: he is the Wisp's summoner.

Its three red lights spiral down to this dark figure who stands on the bank of the frozen river, watching. As the Wisp approaches, with a sudden, swift movement, the man sweeps off his coat and turns it inside out. It is a centuries-old mortal protection against the Wisp's power

— at least for those who know of it. The red lights falter in their approach. The ward may be simple, but it is effective.

The man holds up a forbidding hand. His breath plumes in the air around his head as he speaks. His voice is firm and unafraid.

'I will not follow.'

Now other figures step from out of the black shadows beneath the towering viaduct. The first is a woman with a burnished tumble of red hair like a vixen's tail. She is joined by three others: two men and another woman. All of them are magic-users, all have power at their command. Together they form the sorcerer's coven. The red-haired woman and her companions move to stand behind the sorcerer, their backs deliberately turned away from the glimmering red lure of the Will o' the Wisp.

Its lights cease their swarming dance. They pause before the magician and then merge. As one, the lights become a floating, disembodied head — a head with three twisted, leering inhuman faces. Each has beady black eyes and protruding fangs, a creased forehead and long, pointed ears. The triple-faced head still glows with an ominous red light.

The magician speaks to the three demonic faces.

'I have summoned you for a task, Will O' the Wisp.'

The head nods slowly in response.

'And what –?'

'– What is it –?'

'– You wish us to do?'

'The last chime child must be defeated. There must be no more interference with the Shadowing, or with my plans.' *The sorcerer smiles faintly.* 'My task is one you should enjoy. You are to lure the child to our coven.'

The mortal magician is right – the merest mention of the word 'lure' sets the red glow pulsing about the Wisp's three ugly faces. Three matching, hideous grins of anticipation stretch three demonic sets of lips.

'Seek out the chime child,' *the magician continues,* 'but do not yet attempt to lead him . . . astray. You will not succeed in that without our assistance – the boy's powers are too strong, and he will resist. Seek him out for us, and we will use you as a vessel by which to work our magic, to weaken and confuse him. And then –'

'Then then THEN?' the triple faces cry in frenzy.

The magician chuckles. 'Then you may make your game of him.'

'Very well,' say the heads obediently.

'We will do as you ask –'

'– We will seek out the chime child.'

The magician nods with satisfaction. Behind him, the members of his coven still stand with their backs resolutely turned. So they do not see the demon's triple-faced floating head dissolve again into the three red lights like dancing stars, brightly burning on their way as they sail out into the night.